"I'll tell you nothing," Ki spat. He would not allow Patetta to steal his dignity or to make him reveal *anything* about Jessie.

"That is too bad for you. Do you believe in God, sir? Surely you will tell me that."

"I believe in the gods of my people. Those gods are strong, as are my people. We have never been conquered."

"A martial spirit. I admire it in you, sir," the priest went on. "Well, I am telling you, you will be praying to your gods before the day is out. For, sir, I shall extract the information I want from you—by whatever means necessary."

Also in the LONE STAR series
from Jove

LONGARM AND THE LONE STAR LEGEND
LONE STAR ON THE TREACHERY TRAIL
LONE STAR AND THE OPIUM RUSTLERS
LONE STAR AND THE BORDER BANDITS
LONE STAR AND THE KANSAS WOLVES
LONE STAR AND THE UTAH KID
LONE STAR AND THE LAND GRABBERS
LONE STAR IN THE TALL TIMBER
LONE STAR AND THE SHOWDOWNERS
LONE STAR AND THE HARDROCK PAYOFF
LONE STAR AND THE RENEGADE COMANCHES
LONE STAR ON OUTLAW MOUNTAIN
LONE STAR AND THE GOLD RAIDERS
LONGARM AND THE LONE STAR VENGEANCE
LONE STAR AND THE DENVER MADAM
LONE STAR AND THE RAILROAD WAR
LONE STAR AND THE MEXICAN STANDOFF
LONE STAR AND THE BADLANDS WAR
LONE STAR AND THE SAN ANTONIO RAID
LONE STAR AND THE GHOST PIRATES
LONE STAR ON THE OWLHOOT TRAIL
LONGARM AND THE LONE STAR BOUNTY
LONE STAR ON THE DEVIL'S TRAIL
LONE STAR AND THE APACHE REVENGE
LONE STAR AND THE TEXAS GAMBLER
LONE STAR AND THE HANGROPE HERITAGE
LONE STAR AND THE MONTANA TROUBLES
LONE STAR AND THE MOUNTAIN MAN

WESLEY ELLIS

LONE STAR AND THE STOCKYARD SHOWDOWN

A JOVE BOOK

LONE STAR AND THE STOCKYARD SHOWDOWN

A Jove Book/published by arrangement with
the author

PRINTING HISTORY
Jove edition/October 1984

ISBN: 0-515-07920-0

Jove books are published by The Berkley Publishing Group,
200 Madison Avenue, New York, N.Y. 10016. The words
"A JOVE BOOK" and the "J" with sunburst are trademarks
belonging to Jove Publications, Inc.

PRINTED IN THE UNITED STATES OF AMERICA

Chapter 1

A curse split the air, and the Oriental man looked across the room from the comfortable leather chair he was sitting in. At a vast desk in the corner, the woman slammed down a large ledger book in disgust. She rose and shoved her chair away and spoke to the man.

"Ki, I hate this—this toting up numbers. It never works out the way I want it to. Maybe I wasn't born to be a businesswoman."

"You were born to be your father's daughter, Jessie. That includes bookkeeping work as well as riding the range. You have very little choice in the matter."

"Well, I'm going to hire an accountant to keep these blasted books. I'm sick of it." Jessica Starbuck strode across the high-ceilinged, book-lined study. It had been one of her father's favorite rooms in the big house he had built when she was a small girl. Because of the memories it brought back, it was one of her favorite rooms, too—except when she had to do bookkeeping chores for the ranch operation.

"You are the boss. You can hire whomever you please," said Ki. "If you loathe the numbers that much—"

"Look at my fingers," she said petulantly, holding up the ink-stained digits. "Who needs it?" She sat down hard on the arm of Ki's chair and folded her arms. Her eyebrows were knit in serious dissatisfaction.

A handsome, almond-eyed man of Japanese and American parentage, Ki looked up at Jessie appraisingly. Her golden red hair cascaded to her shoulders, framing a frank, beautifully constructed face. Her pursed lips were red, her nose softly upturned, her green eyes burning with impatience. He had to laugh.

She glared at him. "What's so funny? I'd like to see you try—"

But Ki could not contain his mirth. Then it struck Jessie and her frown melted and she began laughing, too.

"I know—I'm a spoiled brat who can't take a little ink on her precious fingers. Darn it, Ki, you're making fun of me."

"No, just enjoying your discomfort. Forgive me, Jessie, but I know you so well."

"Too well, if you ask me," the young woman said, pushing herself upright. "And you—you inscrutable son of a prairie dog, you think it's so funny. All right, I'm a pampered young bitch who's had everything on a silver platter. The funny thing is, I'd rather be out riding with the others, overseeing the fall roundup."

"You have a foreman to do that for you," Ki replied.

"Maybe I should make him stay here and do the books, and then I could take over the foreman's job. I wouldn't mind trading places with him."

"Roundup is nearly finished," Ki observed. "They'll be

branding the calves and preparing the steers for shipping north. You should have thought of this weeks ago." The chastisement was laced with a heavy dose of affection. This eager, impatient young woman was the best friend he had; her life was his.

"Why are you always right, Ki?" she asked.

"Not always. Most of the time."

"Well, I find it infuriating," Jessie said with a genuine smile.

"Myobu is preparing some tea. It will calm you down."

"But will it solve my problem, Ki? Tea isn't the answer to everything, you know."

Jessie's problem would be the envy of any cattle rancher: this year she would enjoy a record gather for autumn, almost six hundred head more than had been originally estimated. It had been an exceptional summer and her herd had thrived; even she was at a loss to explain the bounty. And now she was faced with trying to find a big enough market to handle all this Circle Star beef.

She brightened at the prospect; it meant that she would have to take personal charge of bringing the beef to market. She turned again to Ki.

"I'm going to Kansas City, my friend. That'll be just the thing for me. I'll hire someone to look after the books here, and I'll go with the herd. We have to cut a new deal for all those extra head. Now that's my idea of fun—that might calm me down for a while."

Ki sighed. "I'm glad the railroad has anticipated you, Jessie. I can't see you eating dust on a cattle drive."

"Me too," she agreed. "We'll ride north in comfort—and so will our cattle. I've not been to Kansas City for a long time. Not since I was a little girl." She clapped her hands, relishing the thought of a new adventure. "I bet I can get a good sale there. I hear the town is booming."

Ki shrugged. "If you can't sell cattle in Kansas City, you can't sell them anywhere."

Jessie's eyes were alight. She returned to the desk. "You're right again, Ki. And that gives me another idea." She pulled a sheet of writing paper from the drawer and re-inked her pen and began scribbling.

Ki contemplated the scene. This volatile, impatient, infuriatingly beautiful young woman had just a moment ago been complaining about her stained fingers: now she was back with pen in hand and a new idea in her head. He waited for her to finish whatever she was writing.

As he watched her, his heart brimming with love for her, Ki's mind stepped back in time. His years of samurai training had disciplined his body, his soul, and his mind so that he could remember people and events—in accurate detail—whenever he chose to. Now a picture came to him—a picture of Jessie Starbuck as a honey-haired girl, sitting in this very room while her father did *his* paperwork at the same desk where she sat today.

In those days Jessie had been a happy, active girl, even though she no longer had a mother. In fact, her mother had been killed many years previously, almost before Jessie had had a chance to form an impression of that beautiful, vibrant woman who had captured Alex Starbuck's heart. From an early age, Jessie had been the woman of the house, and she was rarely far from her father's side when he was home at the Circle Star. Her life was entwined with his in a way that made her, even at such an early age, a clear reflection of one of the most powerful men in Texas.

For Jessie's father was not only a top cattleman, but a man with wide-ranging business interests that comprised holdings all over the American West and abroad. A veteran world traveler, Alex Starbuck had been one of the first Americans to land in Japan, where, as a young man, he had begun to develop an appreciation for that foreign culture—and to see the vast possibilities of trade with the mysterious island people.

Over the years he continued to build on that experience

and acumen, forming business contacts in San Francisco, New York, and Washington, as well as in the capital cities of Europe and Asia. The name Starbuck became well known and well respected in business circles all around the globe. His headquarters, though, and the place he loved best, was in West Texas—the Circle Star spread, which he had built up in a hostile wilderness to be one of the most profitable cattle operations in the state. This was the one place he had really called home—until his death.

Then, in the prime of his life, Alex Starbuck had been murdered—brutally assassinated by gunmen hired by a group of European businessmen, most of them Prussian, who had wanted Starbuck out of the way; he was *too* successful in their eyes, providing too much direct competition in the international sphere. These men, ruthless enough to pay for another man's death, had sworn to fight Jessie's father—and that was exactly what they had done and they fought dirty. She hated every one of them, and she had vowed to avenge her father's death. Over the past months and years she had devoted herself almost exclusively to that cause, and had hurt the cartel time and again. It was a testament to Jessie's—and Ki's—resourcefulness that she was still alive.

It wasn't that Jessie enjoyed killing; in fact, she loathed taking the life of another human being. But she was wise enough from experience—if still young in years—to know that a blood debt must be paid in blood, and that her father, while not condoning them, would understand the necessity of her actions. She had loved her father so much in life, and she respected his memory so much in death, that she was willing to pay the highest price of all for him—her own life, which was constantly on the line.

As for Ki, who was watching her now as she committed her idea to paper, he had an equal investment—emotional and spiritual—in Jessie's cause. Alex Starbuck had been as close to him, too, as a father. Those years flashed before him now, those years he had worked with Alex and learned to honor the man. The cartel's minions were cowards, he knew, because they had killed their enemy in an ambush, backshooting him, allowing him no chance to defend himself. These were not warriors, who observed the proprieties of armed combat; they were more like the *ninja,* the assassins of the night, who slit a man's throat when he was sleeping. Ki hated these men and, like Jessie, had sworn to destroy them for what they had done.

Together, Jessie Starbuck and Ki made a formidable fighting team, which their enemies often underrated. Whenever they encountered members or representatives of the cartel—which they frequently did, for the cartel had vast interests throughout the United States and its territories—they were able to use their keen talents successfully against unsuspecting opponents, keeping the cartel off guard and always on the defensive.

It had been a long while, though, since they had run up against an arm of the cartel. For the past summer they had been occupied at the Circle Star, seeing to it that the herd prospered, and preparing for the fall roundup.

Jessie looked up at Ki with a glint of triumph in her eyes. "Listen to this," she said to him. "Tell me if you think it's a brilliant idea or not."

She held up the piece of paper. "It's a letter to Jason Weatherby in Kansas City. He's president of the United National Bank there.

"'Dear Mr. Weatherby, I am writing to inform you that I shall be in Kansas City on business within the next three weeks. I wish to meet with you at that time to discuss the possibility of my purchasing an interest in a stockyard operation in your city. Because my ranch, the Circle Star, has shown a surplus this season, I shall be able to sell at a high profit. Therefore, I plan to deposit the proceeds from that sale in your bank. Please advise me as to a day and time when you are available to discuss this proposal. Until I receive word from you I shall remain, yours truly . . .' And so on."

Ki listened to her reading of the letter with a smile on his face. He had to give her credit—she had gumption, as the Americans said. He nodded. "It's a very good letter, Jessie. Do you know this man, Jason Weatherby?"

"No, but my father had dealings with him in the past. So he'll know who I am."

"The Starbuck name is famous," he kidded her.

"My father's name is famous," Jessie replied. "I'll never command the widespread attention he did. But that's fine with me. I work best when we can be as inconspicuous as possible."

"That isn't very often," said Ki. "Men tend to pay close attention when you're around."

"Stop it, Ki. You're making fun of me again."

"No, simply telling the truth."

"Well, I don't care if Mr. Weatherby knows I'm Alex Starbuck's little girl. When he sees the money we're going to realize from this cattle shipment, he'll sit up and take notice. That's all the attention I want from him."

"So you really want to buy into a stockyard operation in Kansas City? What made you think of that?"

"I was just thinking—with five or six hundred extra head, will there be enough corral space for them in Kansas City? I figure they have several stockyard operators there—and maybe there's need for another. That's me. And I can provide the stock to fill it twice a year."

"So you will back up your investment with a commitment to provide a certain number of head next year and the following years. You can't lose money that way."

"I'm hoping Weatherby will see it that way, and match my profit with a loan that I can use to buy big. It'll pay for itself in a couple of years."

Jessie seemed convinced that it could work. And she was proud of herself for having thought of the scheme. One thing her father had taught her was that you have to spend money to make money. The family fortune would never grow if she just sat on it, didn't try to put it to work. With the cattle operation a secure base, along with Alex Starbuck's various thriving interests in other Western territories, there was no reason for her to sit tight. Future generations of the family—if ever there were any—had to be kept in mind.

Ki said, "I think it's a good thing. I'll want to be there when this banker meets you for the first time."

"He'll see how much sense it makes," she said confidently. "It's a good idea. I feel it in my bones." She stood up from the desk. "At least it wasn't a wasted afternoon. I thought I was going to go crazy, cooped up in here all day with this paperwork."

"One day, all of America will be run by men who do nothing but put numbers on paper," Ki declared.

"Why do you say that?" she asked.

"Already men in New York, the men who control the money, are that way. And you know how your capital city, Washington, works. In those marble buildings are hundreds of men with eyeshades on, bent over their little desks and governing this country on paper. So don't despair of all the hours you spend mastering the use of the pen."

She laughed. "I'll try not to. But I really can't believe this country will ever be like that, just a lot of dry little people forever juggling numbers and shuffling papers."

"Maybe not," he said, and stood and stretched. "In any case, I think you've done enough of it for now. Let's have that tea."

Fifteen days later, Jessie and Ki accompanied several thousand head of prime beef to Kansas City, Missouri. They rode the shining new rail line from West Texas that cut up through the Indian Nations and Kansas to their ultimate destination. It had been a long time since Jessie had spent so many hours on a train, and she tried to distract herself with a book. But the excitement of the challenge that faced her—putting together the financing for a stockyard operation—occupied her mind for most of the trip.

She had not heard from the banker, Weatherby, in reply to her letter. This didn't worry her, but she was curious as to why the Starbuck name had not brought a prompt written response. She looked out the train window at the stark, flat Kansas plain, and she felt the first faint foreboding that something was wrong.

Turning to Ki, she said, "We'll be there by nightfall. And I'll be glad to stretch my legs."

The silent samurai, who had sat near her for the long trip, said, "I will be, too."

He looked at her as she stared out through the grimy, soot-streaked glass at the open land. It was past noon, and the sun shone golden from a cloudless sky upon the vast stretches of browning grass. Ki estimated that they had four hours more to travel. Nothing would please him better than being rid of this infernally cramped railroad compartment. He was tall for his race—because his father had been an American—and he could find no comfortable position in which to ride. He much preferred a horse as a means of travel, as did Jessie.

Ki swung his legs out into the narrow lane between his seat and Jessie's. He was wearing a black cotton shirt, denim trousers, and rope-soled slippers. Beneath the black shirt he carried a short-bladed *tanto* knife, the only weapon on his person. He stood and moved toward the door of the compartment. The train swayed, but Ki walked with the lithe grace of a cat, keeping his balance.

"It's like a coffin, this place," he said. "I must open the door for a moment, Jessie."

"Go ahead. I feel the same way," she said absently, gazing at the distant blue horizon. "I could use a glass of wine, Ki."

"I will not leave you alone, Jessie. We can call for a porter."

"Oh, Ki, you worry too much. Nothing's going to happen to me on this train. Please, see if you can find me some wine—or something. I'm thirsty."

Ki was about to protest, but he thought better of it. He could use a walk, and if she wanted some wine, he might as well get her some. He'd be gone only two or three minutes. So he said, "Don't let anybody else in. I'll lock the door."

She nodded, thanking him. She opened her book once again.

The dining area was three cars toward the front of the train, and Ki made his way there. Just as he reached the dining car, the train lurched to a stop, wheels grinding and brakes shrieking. He went to the window and looked out to see why they had stopped. What he saw out there made his blood run cold.

At the front of the train, six or eight stray cattle were grazing on or near the railroad tracks. It looked to Ki as if it were no accident that the cows were there, for he saw two horses, saddled but riderless, grazing there as well. He looked back toward the car from which he had come—where Jessie was. He saw nothing.

It didn't seem right. What was going on? Following his first instinct, the samurai turned and retraced his steps. Throughout the cars, passengers were sticking their heads out from their compartments and milling in the narrow passageway, blocking Ki. He had to push through them. His heart was pounding faster, the closer he got to his car. He cursed himself for his carelessness, a momentary lapse—but at exactly the wrong time. Leaping into the car just as the train began to move again, Ki was at the compartment in three steps.

There he saw the reason for the unscheduled stop. Two

men were trying to break in. As he reached them, they broke open the fragile door and burst into the small cabin. Ki reached for the closest man, a bull-shouldered fellow in a floppy brown hat. Snaking his arm around the man's neck, Ki jerked him back out through the shattered door.

Inside, Jessie reacted quickly, her converted .38 Colt filling her hand from its hiding place on the seat beside her. She looked at the intruder, a pale, unshaven, hatchet-faced man with dull black eyes. Raising her revolver, she saw the man pause for just a second.

"Who the hell are you?" she demanded. The man stared dumbly, surprised at her spunk. She began to rise from her seat, leveling the gun at his chest.

The man moved more quickly than she had expected. His right hand whipped out, knocking the Colt from her hand. The weapon fell on the opposite seat with a thud. Now the intruder took a half-step toward her, unholstering a big revolver of his own. Jessie ducked and reached for her gun. The man growled, "Don't try it, missy—or I'll blow that pretty head off."

Outside, in the narrow passageway, Ki swung a hard forearm into his opponent's Adam's apple, stunning the man. He followed with a quick knee into the man's thick midsection. All the air whooshed out of the man's lungs but, bent over, he charged at Ki, taking the samurai in the groin with his hard head.

Ki tried to avoid the blow, but there was nowhere to move. Confined in these close quarters, he had to take the pain. The man was like a crazed bull, charging blindly. Ki forced his head down and leapfrogged over the man. Then he turned and planted his heel in the man's ass, shoving him away. The man crashed headfirst into the door at the end of the car and crumpled in a heap there.

Swinging in through the gaping door to help Jessie, Ki was met with a twelve-inch steel barrel in his gut. The tall man, who had disarmed Jessie, caught Ki low in the belly, using the gun barrel like a dull ax blade to drive the samurai back against the wall.

Pain stabbed up and down the length of his spine as Ki slammed back, and he felt his knees buckle.

Jessie dove again for her .38-caliber revolver. She grabbed the gun butt and brought it around again, lying horizontally across the seat. The tall attacker was right in front of her. She heard the click of his gun as he cocked it. Then a loud roar filled her ears. Rolling quickly to her left, she felt the hot blast of the bullet as it chewed into the seat cushion, burning a big hole there.

Dropping to her knees, Jessie raised the Colt yet again, this time squeezing off a shot. Her nostrils filling with acrid powdersmoke, she saw that she had only clipped a wing as the man reached for his shoulder wound.

Behind the attacker, Ki was roused by the gun blast. He shook his head to clear it, and sprang into action. He tackled the tall man, crushing his knees in a powerful arm clasp and yanking his feet from under him. The man fell, but he still kept hold of his long-barreled gun. He had time to pull off another round that snapped past Jessie's ear. In the thick gunsmoke, Jessie looked for Ki. She saw him as he brought the tall, ugly man down. Then she looked up, beyond Ki, to see another figure looming at the door: the second attacker. His wide frame filled her vision, as did the pistol in his thickfingered hand.

Without hesitation, Jessie aimed and fired, loosing a bullet that ripped into the stocky intruder's chest. The man drew a stunned breath, then spat a mouthful of blood as his lungs collapsed and he gripped the doorframe for support.

"Ki!" Jessie shouted through the smoke and blood mist.

"Stand back!" he called to her as he forced the taller man over on his stomach and held the bony hands together. With a leather cord, the samurai secured the man's wrists. He stood up and surveyed the unpleasant scene.

"My God!" Jessie breathed. "Who are these men?"

Ki said, "They stopped the train in order to get at you. They knew where you were."

Puzzled, Jessie sat back down on the undamaged seat. She looked at the man she had injured; he was still alive, but probably in shock now, and bound helplessly. Ki stood over him. Something in the corner of her eye made her look up toward the door.

There, the stocky man's body moved. She had thought he was dead. For a second she didn't realize what he was doing. Then she saw the gun in his hand.

"Ki!" she began. "That one's still alive!"

Ki turned, reaching for his *tanto* blade, freeing it, holding it poised in his slender fingers.

The man at the door looked up, his eyes bloodshot, his mouth open. He looked at Ki, but his gunhand was extended toward his partner. He was going to kill the other attacker to keep him from talking.

Ki flipped the knife with a powerful wrist, just as the stocky man pulled the trigger. A final explosion rang out; a bullet shattered the tall man's skull and smoke curled from the muzzle of the gun. Ki's *tanto* blade had sliced cleanly through the man's windpipe and severed an artery there, which fountained blood.

Jessie gulped down the contents of her stomach, which were threatening to come up. She averted her eyes from the gore and reached out for Ki, who took her in his arms. He held her tightly. Her heart was pounding violently.

Always, she was prepared to meet danger—it had become a part of her life, following her wherever she went. But the suddenness of this attack, by anonymous men, in the middle of nowhere, on a train—she had not been prepared for it, for the viciousness of it. Thank God for Ki, was all she could think.

Outside their compartment they heard voices. Other passengers had emerged into the passageway. A woman screamed and someone shouted for the conductor. It took several minutes for Ki to clear the people away so that the conductor could enter the cabin.

Stepping over the body sprawled in the door, the blue-uniformed, bespectacled man said, "What have we here?" He appeared nonplussed by the appearance of the gory corpses.

Jessie said, "These men attacked us."

"They'll not attack anyone again very soon," the conductor said.

Jessie did not understand the man's casual attitude. "This is *your* train, sir. You and the railroad are responsible for what happened here."

"I assure you, madam, I know full well who bears responsibility for anything that happens on this train." He was a young man with a smooth face, and his glasses were wire-framed. His mouth was an unexpressive, thin-lipped line.

"What do you intend to do about it, then?" she blazed.

"I shall remove these unsightly bodies and find you another cabin, madam," he said matter-of-factly.

Jessie looked over at Ki. He was watching the conductor intently. She could tell that he was studying the man's behavior.

Later, when their luggage had been moved to a new compartment, on a car closer to the front of the train, Jessie and Ki tried to puzzle out the meaning of the surprise attack. They found that the more they thought about it, the less sense it made.

"How could they have known, Ki?" Jessie wondered aloud. "We didn't tell anybody of our plans until the last minute; we didn't even know which car we'd be on."

"The only man who knows we're coming is the banker, Jason Weatherby. You wrote him over two weeks ago, remember?"

"Of course I remember. But why would he have anything to do with this? We're going to be giving him some good business in Kansas City. He has no reason to want us dead. On the contrary, he stands to lose money if we die before our cattle are safely delivered."

"I didn't like that conductor," Ki said. "He seemed almost to expect trouble."

"Maybe he's seen too much of it. This probably wasn't the first shooting he's witnessed."

"But there wasn't an ounce of surprise or fear in him. He was like a cold fish."

"I have to admit he was, Ki," she said, shaking her head. Still, she couldn't imagine that he was in any way involved. The two attackers could have told them the why and the wherefore of the deed—but they were colder than cold fish by now.

Jessie smoothed her shining hair and felt the need for a hot bath. When they got to Kansas City, off the train and into the hotel, she could take a nice long soak and wash away the unclean feeling of the afternoon.

"I knew I shouldn't have left you alone," Ki said quietly.

"Don't blame yourself," she replied. "You're always by my side when I need you."

"You must be especially careful in town, Jessie, until we know who these men were and why they came after you."

"We'll be there soon," she said.

Outside, the evening sun painted the western sky bright purple and flaming red. The train, clacking along the steel rails, carried them closer to the city. Several cars behind them, the Circle Star herd rode in crowded cattle cars, prime cattle, the product of Jessie's own sweat and brains, hurtling toward the giant corrals where they would await their final journey to the slaughterhouse. The beauty of the sunset and the morbid, sickening thought of the slaughter were mingled in Jessie's mind as she gazed out the train window once again.

Business had been the original purpose of this trip—not

trouble. But Jessie was beginning to wonder whether she could escape the notion that, for her, business almost always meant trouble. She closed her eyes and tried to catch a little sleep.

Chapter 2

The next morning, after a cup of strong coffee and a light breakfast, Jessie and Ki went to the United National Bank to see Jason Weatherby. The bank building was only a few blocks from their hotel, right in the heart of town. Kansas City, at this hour, was alive with activity. The wide streets were populated by businessmen and cowboys, shopgirls and matrons, blacks and Mexicans, all moving purposefully in the bright early sunshine of a new day. This part of town, the business district, boasted several tall buildings—four stories or more—with elegant façades that fronted the clean, paved streets. Vehicles of all sorts—from one-horse buggies to lumbering farm wagons—clogged the thoroughfares, creating a density and a racket that confirmed in a visitor's mind that this was indeed a thriving young city.

Jessie loved the feeling of walking along the sidewalk among the busy crowds. For her it was a different experience, accustomed as she was to the wide spaces and open skies of West Texas. She would never live in a big town like Kansas City—too many folks piled one on top of another, not enough room to breathe—but she liked an occasional visit such as this to get her heart pumping and to see the multiplicity of human faces on display. She, too, of course, received her own share of interested looks, as did her companion.

For her meeting with Weatherby, Jessie had donned a long blue serge skirt and a frilly white blouse with a high collar, and she wore a gray knit shawl and a small blue hat that set off her flaming hair. The one touch of regularity was the pair of riding boots she wore beneath the skirt; she hated the high-heeled, buttoned shoes that so many so-called fashionable women were wearing these days. Who needed the discomfort, just to conform to the fashion of the moment? Such things mattered little to Jessie. She had a strong streak of Starbuck nonconformity in her—another legacy of her father.

Ki, on the other hand, was dressed more conventionally than he had been in a long time. He wore a white shirt, black trousers, and boots. He had on his many-pocketed leather vest, and an American-style Stetson hat. He and Jessie had decided that he would fit in more easily at the bank by forgoing his common mode of dress. He did not like the idea—to him, these clothes were uncomfortable and awkward—but he knew that for this occasion it was best.

Thus the pair were able to walk to the bank without attracting too much unwanted attention. Jessie knew that she would always turn men's heads, and that Ki would often be the focus of hostile stares—but today she did not want to invite the notice of strangers. Today she had important business to conduct, with a minimum of fuss.

"So what do you think of Kansas City?" she asked her companion.

The samurai shrugged. "It is a place with a lot of people. I suppose it is not much different from other cities. It's not as big as Edo or New York, but it might be someday." As they rounded a busy corner, he pointed to a new building being constructed. "It's a growing city, that's for certain."

"I kind of like it," Jessie mused aloud. "It reminds me of Chicago—but not as cold."

Ki smiled. "Sometimes, I hear, Chicago can get very hot."

"Let's hope they don't have a fire like that here," she rejoined. "We won't be around very long, in any case. I hope Weatherby will agree to my proposition this morning so that we can conclude a purchase within the next couple of days."

"Bankers are cautious men," he said.

"Caution I don't mind, especially with *my* money. Since I want to spend it, though, he should be able to help me."

"We'll see," said Ki. Already he was thinking ahead to the afternoon, when he and Jessie would, he hoped, finalize the sale of the Circle Star herd. Those thousands of head would bring a nice price, so Jessie wasn't talking through her hat when it came to money.

At the front of the bank building, Jessie stopped and turned to Ki. "I was just thinking about those two men on the train. I wonder who—" She did not finish the question that had been on her mind through the night.

Ki understood. "We will find out, Jessie. And as I said, we will punish whoever is responsible."

Inside the ornate offices of the United National Bank, Jessie and Ki were directed to the president's suite, which required a ride in a glass-encased elevator to the third floor of the building. Jessie marveled at the laziness of people who needed this little car to take them up two flights, when a short walk up a staircase would get them there as easily.

But a newfangled elevator showed just how prosperous the bank was; she supposed it went with the territory.

Weatherby's secretary, a pretty blond girl who sat at a desk outside the bank president's inner office, told them that he had a visitor at present and suggested that they have a seat in the waiting area.

Several minutes ticked by, and then the big door opened soundlessly and a man emerged. Dressed in a long, crow-black soutane with a Roman collar, and a biretta atop his head, the man was easily identifiable as a Catholic priest. He had a smooth, clean-shaven white face, an aquiline nose, and heavy black brows. He did not acknowledge Jessie and Ki as he strode majestically out, ramrod-stiff, in a whisper of black cloth.

The secretary announced Jessie and Ki, who made their way into Weatherby's sanctum. Lavishly furnished in dark red leather and gleaming wood, the president's office was a large, high-ceilinged room, dominated by a massive desk of carved oak, behind which stood Jason Weatherby.

He came around to greet Jessie with an outstretched hand. "Miss Starbuck, it is a pleasure to make your acquaintance. I had many dealings with your father before his, his untimely passing. Allow me to add my condolences as well, even at this late date."

"Thank you," Jessie said, shaking his hand. "This is my partner, Ki," she continued. "He worked for my father and is an invaluable friend."

Jessie sized up Weatherby as he gave a brief, firm shake to Ki's hand. The banker looked to be about fifty years old, with a shock of iron-gray hair combed straight back from his angular, creased face. Sidewhiskers, also gray, outlined his strong upper jawline; his dark eyes flashed in Jessie's direction, and his wide, thin-lipped mouth curled in a smile.

The banker was tall—about six feet—and trim, with wide shoulders and long arms. He stooped slightly but moved without hesitation, inviting his two visitors to sit as he returned to his own chair behind the desk. He was dressed simply but expensively in a charcoal-gray suit, a white shirt with a stiff collar, and a black cravat pinned to his breast with a white pearl. He took a long cigar from a box and sniffed it before sitting back and striking a match.

"What may I do for you, Miss Starbuck?" he asked between puffs. A cloud of smoke obscured his face.

Jessie said, "Didn't you receive my letter? I outlined my intentions in it. I wanted to confirm the arrangement today. You didn't answer my letter."

"But I did," Weatherby said. "Perhaps you didn't receive it before you left Texas. The mail service in this part of the country leaves a lot to be desired."

"Well, what do you think of my proposal?" she asked. She felt that direct questions and direct answers were the most economical means of conversation.

"To tell you the truth, Miss Starbuck, I haven't had much time to consider it. In fact, in my letter to you I advised you that this was not a good time to discuss your proposed business, because I'm occupied with a rather time-consuming client who is in town for the week."

Jessie didn't know what to make of Weatherby's ambiguous reply. Was he trying to put her off? "We're talking about quite a bit of money, Mr. Weatherby. I can't believe you consider a few hundred thousand dollars inconsequential."

"I do not. Which is why I had hoped we could discuss the matter at greater length when I have more time to devote to it." He blew a stream of smoke at the ceiling. "It's not a bad plan. In fact, my institution has major interests in several stockyard operations here in Kansas City."

"Then there isn't very much to discuss. I simply want to buy into an operation myself. Nothing complicated about that."

"Of course not. But you want to be sure you are buying into the right operation. That, I trust, is where I come in—

advising you on the wisest place to put your money. To that end, I have ordered my bookkeepers to prepare a report to me on all the properties in which we own interests. That report will not be available for a few days. I'm afraid I must beg your indulgence."

The humble, polite request sounded strange coming from this man. Jessie guessed that he did not talk this way with men—with his usual clients. But she was a woman, as Weatherby could doubtless see, and therefore could be set aside for more pressing business. She didn't like the way he was smiling at her, either.

"Mr. Weatherby," she said, "I didn't come all the way to Kansas City just to be put off. There are other banks in town, and if you can't help me, I shall go elsewhere." She just barely contained her anger.

Ki sat rigidly in his chair beside her, and did not take his gaze off Weatherby. He didn't like what he was hearing any more than she did.

"What can I say?" the banker intoned. "Certainly I wish you to bring your business to me. I consider it an honor to work with your family." He consulted a gold pocket watch.

He seemed to consider the situation for a moment. Then he said, "I'll tell you what, Miss Starbuck—I'll meet with you the day after tomorrow, after I've had a chance to look at my people's report. Please be assured that I do not want to lose your account—but it is truly an inconvenient time for me."

Weatherby raised his hands in a gesture of futility and kept the ingratiating smile on his face. To Jessie, this behavior just didn't add up, but she relented.

"All right," she said. "The day after tomorrow. But if you can't give me a definite answer then, I must consider going somewhere else."

"Understood," Weatherby replied. "I appreciate your patience, and I'm sure we can work something out. This is a wide-open town, as the newspaper writers say. A young woman such as yourself could go far here."

"All I want is a stockyard interest that will not lose money, Mr. Weatherby. I don't want to buy all of Kansas City."

Smoke curled from the banker's nostrils. For a man too busy to act upon her proposal, he was certainly talking a lot. Jessie looked at Ki and they both rose together.

"I am staying at the Hotel President," she stated. "You can reach me there. Thank you for your time."

"Thank you for coming. I wish my letter had reached you before you made this long trip," Weatherby said, coming around to the front of the imposing oak desk.

"We would have come anyway," she said. "We have a lot of cattle to sell."

"I take it the gather was a particularly bountiful one," said Jason Weatherby. "You are to be congratulated on that. I'm sure your father would be proud of his daughter, to see her running a profitable ranch."

"When I set out to do something, I do the best I can," Jessie stated flatly. "Goodbye for now, Mr. Weatherby."

"A real pleasure, Miss Starbuck, Mr. Ki. We'll have much to talk about in two days. Don't spend all your profits in the meanwhile." It was a lame attempt at a joke, but Jason Weatherby was polished enough to get away with it. He squeezed her hand one last time.

Jessie withdrew her hand, feeling uneasy. She couldn't figure this man out. On the surface he was a handsome, smooth-talking, urbane man with his finger on the financial pulse of this thriving city, yet there was something . . . *false* about him. She did not look forward to their next meeting.

In contrast to the plush, masculine elegance of the banker's office, the holding pens downtown near the railroad station were dusty and smelled distinctly unpleasant. The animals bawled loudly, crowded by the hundreds into the pens, with no place to move. Jessie, having changed at the hotel into her "working clothes"—denim trousers and a dark cotton blouse that allowed her more freedom of movement—was talking with one of the Circle Star top hands who had come along on this trip. They almost had to shout above the noise of thousands of milling steers and an arriving train.

The hand told her that the entire Circle Star herd was accounted for and ready to sell. In fact, he said, a man had been by that morning, inquiring about Jessie's beeves.

Gratified that there was already interest, Jessie felt certain that she could make a good sale. She asked her employee who the man was who had made the inquiry.

The hand was about to describe him when he looked up and saw the man coming in their direction. The cowboy pointed to a tall young fellow making his way toward them.

Jessie turned and jumped from the corral rail she had been standing on. The man approached her. He was young—about Jessie's own age—and very brawny, his well-muscled shoulders straining at the fabric of his shirt. He wore a wide-brimmed sombrero with a flat crown, and work-stained leather chaps covered the front of his trousers. Dust streaked his face, and he wiped at it with a bright yellow handkerchief as he approached, his long boots kicking up dust.

She smiled to herself; she liked the look of this man, whoever he was.

"Excuse me, ma'am, are you Miss Jessie Starbuck?" he called to her. His long strides carried him closer.

"That's me," she replied. She felt small—almost like a little girl—as he looked down at her, removing his hat. He had a full head of curly brown hair that was tousled boyishly. "What can I do for you?"

The young man introduced himself as Patrick Deighton of the Deighton Meat Company. "I was looking at your herd this morning, ma'am. Prime beef interests me, and you have a lot of it, from what I can see. You selling?"

"For the right price, Mr. Deighton," said Jessie. "How

much are you interested in buying?"

"As much as I can get my hands on," he said, his clear gray eyes frank and friendly. He stood with his arms akimbo, surveying the endless rows of holding pens full of her cattle. "Been a slow season for us so far. Haven't seen the quality of years past. But I like the look of the Circle Star beef."

"Thank you," she said. She had split up with Ki earlier, to allow him to look around town—to scout the territory for her, which he did so well. Jessie wished he were here to meet this man; she thought Ki would like him, and she always trusted Ki's judgment of people.

"Pardon me for asking, ma'am," the big man said somewhat shyly, "but is it true that you're the, er, ramrod of this outfit? I mean, you being a lady and all."

Jessie laughed. Deighton was a bit uncomfortable, it seemed, dealing with her. He was obviously more used to trail-toughened and probably unbathed drovers.

"I own the Circle Star, if that's what you mean."

Deighton scratched his head with a big hand. "That's a mighty big piece to own, if you don't mind my saying so." He looked directly into her clear green eyes. He was impressed with this young woman, and his face showed it. "Then you'll be expecting a big price, I suppose."

"Big enough," she said. "What did you have in mind?"

Deighton smiled, showing his strong white teeth. "I hate to talk money amidst all this animal flesh and bawling, ma'am. If you'd like to have supper with me tonight, we could discuss the price. I think I'll need something in my stomach."

"Yes, I'd like that," Jessie said. "But I must tell you that if I receive other bids today, I'll have to consider them too. I'm not leaving here until I get the right price."

"Just don't leave till we've talked," said Deighton.

"I don't plan to. Where shall I meet you?"

"I'll pick you up, wherever you're staying."

"The Hotel President. Seven o'clock?"

"I'll be there, Miss Starbuck." Deighton replaced his hat and strode away.

As she watched him leave, Jessie felt a strange curiosity growing within her. She wanted to know all about this young man; she very much wanted to dine with him, to see him dressed in evening clothes, to hear his proposition. What a contrast, she thought, between Patrick Deighton and the banker, Jason Weatherby. She had felt almost angry and disappointed with Weatherby earlier today, but with young Deighton she felt—well, a lot different.

Chapter 3

Ki saw them as he passed a dark, narrow alleyway on his way back to the hotel. He had made his customary scouting rounds of the city and had found out nothing particularly helpful. Now he stopped and peered into the space between the two tall buildings. He thought he had heard a woman's voice. He moved into the alley stealthily.

As he drew closer he could see a man and a girl. The man had her pinned against a wall, pressing her there with all his force. The girl's face was uplifted and her open mouth was covered by his hand. Ki took two quick steps forward. The man cried out, whipping his hand from her mouth. She had bitten him.

"Leave her alone," Ki said in a cold, even voice.

The man reacted, turning toward the sound of the intruder. Ki stopped ten feet away.

"Who the hell're you?" the man growled, his eyes squinting. Although it was midday, it was dark in this narrow passage, and difficult to see.

But Ki saw the situation clearly enough. The man had ripped the front of the girl's dress off her. She clutched at it, trying unsuccessfully to hold it in place. As the man turned, she slid down and ducked away under his arm, darting deeper into the alley.

"Sonofabitch," the man hissed. "You oughta learn to keep your nose outta other folks' business." He took a step toward Ki. "I'll kill you for this, you—"

"I don't want to fight you," said Ki. "Go away from here and leave the girl alone. That's all I ask."

"All he asks," breathed the man. Then, as he was almost upon Ki, he said, "Why, it's nothin' but a goddamn Chinaman!"

With a lunge, the man tackled Ki. There was no room for him to maneuver, so he went down, crashing to the ground with the man on top of him, nearly knocking the breath out of him.

The man's fetid breath sprayed into Ki's face as he said, "You goddamned yellow nigger—none of your goddamned business—"

Freeing his right hand, Ki drove his stiffened fingers upward into the man's throat. The steel-hard fingertips rammed against his Adam's apple, choking off any further talk. The plug-ugly pushed himself up and grasped his throat, gurgling in pain and surprise.

Using his legs as twin levers, Ki upended the man vertically, tossing him backwards. The man swung like the hand on a clock and landed face-first in the dust with a grunt. Ki scrambled upright and stood with his legs apart, his arms extended and bent slightly at the elbows.

Behind him, Ki heard the girl as she approached again, probably having found no way out of the alley. *"Mein Gott!"* she whimpered. Ki turned and told her to stand back. And in that split second the downed man was back on his feet, charging again at Ki.

Ki felt the impact of the man's body once more, but this time he was better prepared. Having established his own center of gravity, Ki used his assailant's weight against him. Reaching down, the samurai yanked the man's legs off the ground and the attacker went down. This time, however, he was up in a flash, and even angrier than before.

"You yellow sonofabitch, I'm gonna break your goddamn neck!"

Ki ignored the insults, assuming his stance. With lightning quickness, he kicked his left leg forward, scoring a glancing blow to the man's stomach with the ball of his foot. Then he hopped back a few paces and, in a windmilling flurry of arm movement, charged into his opponent. A knife-hand chop caught the man at the side of his neck, while an uppercut, using the heel of his other hand, met the man's chin with a crack. With a clacking of teeth, the man's mouth closed on his tongue. As the attacker staggered back, blood poured from between his lips. He spat it away in a crimson spray.

He could barely talk now. All Ki heard were crude noises that must have been futile curses. The man reeled but held his ground. Ki realized that he had driven the man too far. There would be no truce or surrender. The thug was blood-mad, having been robbed of his chance at the girl and now hurt badly by a slant-eyed stranger.

Ki checked again behind him. He saw the girl, her blond hair scattered over her face, clinging with fright to the wall, holding up her dress. Even in the darkness he could see her eyes wide in terror, and he could almost hear her heart beating wildly.

Then, as he quickly faced the maddened attacker once more, the samurai saw that the man had pulled a foot-long bowie knife.

With a barely visible bloodied leer, the man brandished the knife. "Come and get it," he spat. His shirtfront was spattered with blood from his mouth, but he did not seem to care. All he wanted was to slice Ki up the middle and spill the intruder's blood in this shadowed alley. Then he would have his way with the girl and kill her, too.

Ki knew that he would have to kill the man, or injure him badly, to get out of this mess. He would never understand men who thrived on violence and dishonor. Why they would choose such a life was an unanswerable question, a mystery to him. Tired, but determined to win this encounter, Ki faced the enemy.

"You are a fool," he said.

Enraged, the man advanced, the knife held low, swinging easily in his hand. He would go right for the gut, Ki decided.

With a powerful roundhouse kick, Ki tried to stun the man's opposite shoulder. The man wheeled back, avoiding the blow. Bringing his leg down, Ki spun in a full circle, then took another step forward, kicking with his other leg at the man's kneecap. He kept his upper body back, to stay clear of the big knife. But again the attacker moved fast enough, and escaped without being hit.

Now Ki was becoming angry, but he had to conquer the emotion. He dug deep within himself to call forth his samurai training: *Anger is the chief enemy of the warrior, more powerful in battle than cowardice. Kill without anger, for that is the way of the warrior. Let the enemy die angry as the warrior lives with clear purpose and courage*. The words of his teacher, Hirata, came back to him, and he listened and put aside thoughts that would distract him.

He heard the girl's breathing behind him as he kept his body between her and the attacker. With powerful concentration he stilled his own inner turmoil and infused his heart and limbs with power. Then he moved deliberately to confront the man.

The man grinned as Ki came closer. Holding the handle of the bowie knife in his right hand, he taunted the samurai. "Come in, yellowbelly. I'll do it for you—I'll spill your yellow innards right here. I'll cut out those slanty eyes and eat 'em for supper." The man was crazed, blood still bubbling from his mouth, his words slurred.

Ki advanced another step, keeping his body just out of knife range. He'd finish the man now or never. He was tired of this. His face was a mask of warrior's calmness, his blood ran cold like a mountain stream.

The attacker, with a whiplike swing of his arm, slashed the knife horizontally, barely missing Ki's stomach. Ki brought his right forearm down, smashing into the man's knife wrist—at the same time pushing an open left hand into his face. Ki felt the man's nose collapse under the force of the blow, but the knife remained in his hand. Ki rocked back on one foot, then lifted a knee and delivered it high, into his opponent's ribcage. Stunned, the air rushing out of his lungs, the man staggered back.

Ki reached for the knife hand, gripping it tightly with both of his own hands. He brought the hand against the nearest wall, once, twice, three times, until finally the knife fell to the ground. Reeling back, the man with the bloody face gaped, unbelieving. As Ki approached him, he turned and ran. Ki was about to pursue him when he remembered the girl. He turned back to find her.

She was hugging the wall, sobbing. Ki went to her and touched her shoulder. At first she shrank back from him. Then, coming to her senses and realizing that she was out of danger, she let him hold her, still clutching her torn dress to her breast.

"Don't be afraid," Ki reassured her. "You're safe now."

"Oh—oh—" The girl raised her face to Ki's. In the deep shadows of the alley he could see her tear-streaked cheeks, her wild eyes. *"Danke*—thank you," she said. "I do not know what happened. He—that man—took me here. I was walking on the street." She spoke with an accent that Ki identified as German.

"He's gone now," Ki said soothingly. "He will not harm you."

"Yes, he is gone," she sighed, as if not quite believing it could be true.

"Did he hurt you?" Ki asked.

The girl shook her head, saying softly, "No."

"I think he will not try to attack another woman for a long time," said Ki.

"How can I thank you, Herr—?" She stopped, not knowing what to call him.

"My name is Ki," he said. "What is yours?"

"Heidi. I am not an American. I am visiting this country with my . . ." She searched for the correct word in English. "With my employer."

"Where are you staying? I will take you there."

"Oh—I look so—I cannot go back there like this. I cannot explain to them what happened."

"Can you repair your dress? I'll take you to my hotel and you can do it there. You can also get cleaned up before you return to your employer."

"That would be so nice of you, Herr Ki. I thank you," she said.

"Come, then." Ki took her arm and allowed her to walk as naturally as possible while she held her dress in place.

Luckily they were only a short distance from the Hotel President, and he was able to whisk her through the lobby and upstairs to the second floor where he and Jessie had rooms. He left her in his room and went to find a maid who could provide him with a needle and thread. Within a few minutes he returned with the implements.

He found the girl sitting on his bed, wearing one of his

long silk robes. Her damaged dress was in her lap, and her face was washed, her hair freshly brushed.

She was a stunningly pretty young woman with sparkling blue eyes, high cheekbones, and glossy hair the color of fresh golden straw. She seemed to have recovered almost completely from her ordeal. Greeting him with a shy smile, she said, "I found this housecoat. I hope you do not mind. I had to wear something."

"I am glad you found it." He wanted to say that she looked beautiful in the colorful Japanese robe, but did not. He gave her the needle and thread, and she set to work repairing her dress. Ki sat beside her on the bed as she worked. He said, "What brings you to this city, so far from your home? Does your employer have business here?"

"My employer is His Royal Highness, Prince Klaus von Stumpf. He came to the United States several months ago. He is about to embark upon what they call a Grand Tour of the Great Western States. He wants to see buffaloes and Indians and the great mountains that he has read about in Germany. I am with the Princess's party—that is, Princess Therese. She is a beautiful woman, and a very kind mistress."

"So you've traveled a great distance. It's too bad you got into such an unpleasant situation here. If this were my country, I should be ashamed of it, for that man's behavior."

"Where are you from, Herr Ki? Indeed, you do not look like an American."

"Please just call me Ki. One name is enough for me. I am from the Japans. I was born there. My father was an American and my mother was Japanese. I grew up there and came to America in the employ of Mr. Alex Starbuck. I work for his daughter now, Miss Jessie Starbuck. When we aren't traveling, we live in Texas on her ranch, the Circle Star."

Heidi's brow knit quizzically. "Starbuck...I think I have

heard that name. I'm not certain where, but I have heard it." She smiled, dismissing the idea. "Perhaps I just thought I heard it."

But Ki was not so sure. He trusted the girl's instincts, though he decided not to press her on the point. He said, "Why did the prince come to Kansas City?"

"He has some business here, with one of the banks. Then from here we shall embark on our Grand Tour." Her fingers worked deftly with the cloth and thread.

"Do you know which bank in particular?" Ki asked.

"No, but he is dining with the president of the bank this evening. Father Patetta arranged all that. And Father Patetta will be there, too. I'm glad—it will give me a night away from that man."

"Father Patetta is a priest?"

"Yes. But more than a priest—an adviser to the prince."

"You do not like him?"

"I was always taught to respect men of the Church. In fact, I was raised in a convent, and I've always been a good Catholic—even though there aren't many Catholics in the German states. But Father Patetta is different from other priests I have known. He does not seem the least concerned with God's work—more with making money for the prince."

Ki mulled over what Heidi had said. Was she talking about the same man he and Jessie had seen in Weatherby's office this morning? Was Weatherby the banker dining with the royal couple tonight? And *had* the girl heard Jessie's name in conversation between the priest and the prince? Something didn't quite add up here.

"What does this priest look like?" he asked her.

"Well, Father Patetta isn't a tall man. He is dark, with bushy black eyebrows and a long straight nose. Some of the girls think he is handsome. I don't. I don't like the way he looks at me—not like a priest is supposed to look at a girl."

Ki nodded. "I think I have seen this man. Does he wear a black priest's robe?"

"Yes, all the time. That is, when he is not saying Mass. He has some pretty vestments he wears when saying Mass. Where did you see him?"

"At the offices of the United National Bank this morning. He was just coming from a meeting with the president, Jason Weatherby."

"Yes. Weatherby. That is who the prince will see tonight—and there is to be a large dinner reception tomorrow night. Then we are supposed to begin our tour."

Ki looked at this pretty young woman as she quickly mended her torn dress, wondering what spirit had brought him together with her. He was glad he had been able to save her from her attacker, and pleased also that he had this opportunity to speak with her. Something about this royal party and its priest troubled him. He wished he could somehow get inside Prince von Stumpf's coterie to find out more, and it occurred to him that this girl might provide the opportunity . . . but he dismissed the notion, since it might jeopardize her safety.

Heidi was saying, "I'm sorry that we'll be leaving—since I have met you." Her cornflower eyes were focused dreamily on Ki's handsome olive-complexioned face.

"Are you feeling better?" he asked, to divert her. He did not want to take advantage of her now—not so soon after her encounter with the would-be rapist in the alley.

"Yes, I feel fine," she said. She bit off the thread, finishing the repair job. She held the dress up to inspect it. "That looks not bad," she concluded, admiring it.

"How did you learn such good English?" the samurai wondered aloud.

Heidi laughed—a wonderful, musical sound. "The convent where I was raised was unusual. Many of us girls were trained for work in royal households or in diplomatic missions. We learned many languages. I preferred English, and found it much easier to learn. Not many girls in my country get the opportunity to learn so much. I am grateful to the nuns who took me in and taught me. You see, my mother and father died when I was just four years old. I had nowhere else to go."

"I'm sorry to hear that. I am an orphan, too. I would have died as a boy in Japan if I had not found a man, Hirata, who took me under his wing and taught me. I, too, am grateful that my youth was not wasted."

"We have much in common, Ki, you and I. I am glad I met you, and so glad you came in time to save me from that—that man." A small tear glistened at the corner of her eye. "I don't know what I would have done. He could have—" She broke off.

"That is over," Ki said softly. "You're safe now."

"Oh, Ki!" she exclaimed. She threw her arms around the samurai, clinging to his strength.

Ki held her gently, letting her squeeze him. She was warm and small and smelled fresh, despite her ordeal. Her hair was soft in his face. He felt a strong stirring deep within himself.

The dress fell to the floor as she held on to the man who had saved her from disgrace. She ignored it. It seemed that all she cared about was this man, this unusual-looking Japanese who had found her just in time. Ki tried to guess what was going on in her mind. He tightened his arms around her as her hands came to his chest and she lifted her face to his.

Her lips found Ki's, and she pressed hard against him. Ki tasted the sweet petals and softly explored with his tongue. Heidi opened her mouth slightly to allow him inside. There his tongue met hers and they meshed wetly, jousting now playfully, now savagely. They kissed hotly for several minutes, until Ki had to pull away to catch his breath.

Heidi's eyes shone, and her chest rose and fell. "Ki, I—"

she began. "I want to love you. You are so strong and so gentle. Please—take me." As she spoke, she pulled apart the silken folds of the robe to reveal her nakedness beneath.

His heart skipping, Ki beheld the clean, smooth white skin of her body. Her breasts were small and round, pink-tipped and pushing upright toward him. The robe fell from her shoulders as she stood before him. He watched it whisper to the floor until she stood there completely nude. Her body was deliciously slender, her stomach flat, a patch of soft blond hair flaring in a triangle between her tapering legs.

Ki reached out for her, and she came to him. He lay her down on the bed and she covered her breasts with her arms in a belated gesture of modesty. He smiled. "You are a beautiful woman, Heidi."

"Tell me that I am beautiful, Ki. Tell me that you love me."

Removing his vest and shirt, Ki said, "Any man would appreciate you—if only men would not try to take without asking. Heidi—" He sat on the bed beside her. "I don't want to take from you without your wanting to give. I don't want to force you. You mustn't do this if you don't want to."

She put a finger on his lips. "I want to," she murmured.

In a moment, Ki had taken off his trousers and lay over her. Again they kissed, their lips melding hotly, her hands on his smooth cheeks. Ki allowed his weight to rest gently upon her, feeling the sensuous curves and valleys of her body beneath him. She was warm, fragrant. His loins came to life insistently as he kissed her.

The girl ran her hands down over his shoulders and chest, her fingertips brushing his ridged, muscular upper body. She cooed beneath him as their lips parted, and she opened her deep blue eyes wide to look at him. Her face was flushed now, her cheeks like freshly blooming roses. She reached farther down with her small hands.

"Oh!" she exclaimed, when she found what she had been

searching for. She took Ki's distended sword in her hands. She touched the hot skin, slipping her fingers down along the shaft to its base.

Ki arched his neck and let out a long, deep groan. Those same deft fingers that had sewn the dress were working on him, and he felt intense longing as she played with him.

"Woman," he breathed, "what are you doing?"

She giggled quietly. "I am just finding out what a man you truly are, Ki."

He rolled off her but kept close, pressing his body to her side. His sword stood erect and she could not let go of it. Her hand ran up and down its length and her eyes glittered, fascinated. Ki stroked her pretty face, unable to take his eyes off her. Then his hand glided down to her pert breasts, which he cupped. Her breathing came faster. Ki took one of her nipples between his finger and thumb and pinched lightly. She started, but the look she gave him told him to continue.

The samurai leaned over and kissed her breasts, flicking his tongue over the erect buds and taking them between his lips to suck gently. With his free hand he found the open chamber of her sex and felt the moistness there, her willingness and need, and probed with a strong finger. He was careful not to press too hard at this point, instead allowing her to build slowly. He rubbed her, his finger avoiding direct contact with the throbbing center of her passion.

Heidi warbled her approval, a trilling sound coming from deep inside her throat. She released his blood-engorged shaft and put her arms around his neck, pulling him closer as he explored her nest. Ki felt the wetness grow, and slowly inserted a finger as far as he could into that tight core of her sex. The walls of flesh became more pliable, more welcoming, as he worked his finger in and out. And the girl, her eyes shut tight, gasped with each movement, gripping Ki's neck and shoulders more tightly.

Ki wanted to be sure she was ready to receive him. He

slowly called forth her love juices, lubricating her chamber, stimulating her and reassuring her of his concern for her own pleasure. He inserted a second finger, pushing it in and pulling it out with the other, and Heidi stifled a cry. Her thighs clasped around his hand, then opened again.

Ki kept the slow but steady pace of his work, bringing forth more wetness, causing her to move with the rhythm of his stimulation.

"Ki . . . please stop. I want you . . . to make love to me. Now, please!" she cried.

The samurai heard her through the hot haze of his own arousal. Her body had grown warmer to the touch as she moved against him.

He took his place above her once again. Heidi opened her pale thighs to him, and Ki guided himself carefully, the head of his shaft finding her welcoming center. With one long thrust he was inside. The girl's mouth opened, but no sound came out as she took him. Her fingers dug into Ki's shoulder blades.

Their mouths met, tongues lashing together. Heidi lifted her legs and locked them around Ki's lower back. Moaning, the girl writhed beneath him as he thrust home again and again. His hips moved with a will of their own, it seemed, as his warrior's lance pistoned in and out.

Their bodies moved slickly against each other, lubricated by a film of perspiration. Heidi's flesh was silky smooth and feminine, Ki's body hardmuscled but flexible. They established a rhythm, echoing the ancient love dance of men and women everywhere, in every time. Ki breathed deeply, attempting to still his heart as it beat wildly, wanting to control this beautiful, magical communion and not let it become pure animal lust. He cared for her and did not want to hurt her.

But the girl had other ideas. She said, "Ki, please stop for a moment." He did, and she held him tightly. "Let me get on top," she whispered. "I want to see you better."

The flowery innocence of her pink face had disappeared, and now he beheld the visage of a woman who wanted to be pleasured and was bound to have her way. What could he say?

Carefully, not breaking the link between them, he rolled over on the bed, carrying her with him, until she had assumed her desired position. Her golden locks fell in shining wisps across her face, and her white breasts hung like soft twin moons above him.

He smiled. "Do you like it like this?"

Merrily, she smiled back. "Oh, yes! Now do it to me, Ki. Make me feel like a real woman."

Heidi lifted her hips and brought them down again. Ki's erection was by now steel-hard and steaming with urgency as he felt her sheath move of its own accord above him. He lifted his own hips to meet her movement. Her arms were planted above his shoulders, and Ki gripped her around the waist to better control their lovemaking in this new position. She began moving again.

Then she started bucking wildly, taking every inch of him, pressing down hard and lifting herself until he almost slipped free. Flesh slapped upon flesh—the only sound other than their hot, ragged breath. It was out of control, but neither of them cared.

Suddenly, Heidi cried out, a high-pitched hymn to Eros. Ki felt her inner muscles contracting around his rigid manhood as it slid up and down. Her face glowed and her eyes were clamped shut. "Ki!" she called, as if to a faraway friend. But Ki was right there, beneath her, as her hips continued to rock.

Ki pressed harder, the volcano boiling within him. As she came, he felt himself closer with each stroke. Without warning, he exploded. His essence spurted forth into her, and he lifted himself up to drive it home one more time.

Later, when they had recovered their equilibrium, they lay enfolded in each other's arms. Ki brushed a sweat-plastered strand of hair from the girl's forehead. She opened her eyes and smiled.

Ki nodded. "You are a lovely woman, Heidi. Any man would be fortunate to have you."

"I am the fortunate one," she whispered, kissing his neck. "I hope I will see you again, before you leave Kansas City."

"Something inside me tells me that you came here for a purpose—and I am a part of that purpose. Is that true?"

"Might be," Ki replied. "The priest you told me about—I don't know the truth of him, but what I do know is that he is already, somehow, my enemy."

The girl sat up. "I believe you. If there is any way I can help you . . ."

Ki took her chin in his hand and kissed her. "You will not do anything foolish. If I call upon you, it will be for information, nothing else. I won't allow you to put yourself in danger."

"I don't fear anything as long as you are near."

"You'd better dress and return to your mistress. I have things to do."

"I want *you* to be careful, Ki. If harm should come to you, I will kill the man responsible."

"Foolish talk. But I am happy you feel that way."

"I do," said Heidi. "And nothing you say will change that."

★

Chapter 4

Jessie looked her best for dinner that evening. In a crimson dress of imported silk, she took Deighton's breath away when he came for her. He, in turn, looked a very different man than the one she had met at the corral earlier that day. He wore a black suit that was tailored expertly to fit his large frame, with a snug vest across which hung an intricate gold watch chain. A stiff white collar and smooth gray necktie completed the outfit, and he carried a wide-brimmed black hat.

She could feel his appraising eyes upon her as she allowed him to help her with her wrap and led her out into the street. Yet she did not feel threatened by him in the least. Unlike some men, who devoured her—raped her sometimes—with their eyes, his was an appreciative sort of gaze. And she had to admit that she did not tire of looking at Patrick Deighton, either. The night air was bracing as they walked toward their destination.

"Where are you taking me?" Jessie asked.

"To the Savoy Hotel. They have a fine restaurant there."

Gaslamps illuminated the streets at every corner, casting a dim yellow glow over the passing vehicles and the strolling people. Above, the clear black sky was punctuated with stars. Jessie took a lungful of air; it tasted good.

Deighton took her arm with a large, steady hand and guided her along the sidewalk. She had to fight the impulse that was growing within her. A part of her wanted to turn back and take Deighton to her hotel room and talk to him in the dark—she felt that much for him—but another part of her, the experienced, mature woman, held back; after all, she barely knew this man. Handsome and friendly as he was, perhaps he was not what he appeared to be.

Jessie had often been disappointed in men she had trusted. Too frequently, men thought they could use her for their own ends, as if she were a piece of currency or a commodity. But she had learned to handle herself, to avoid exploitation—indeed, to avoid death at the hands of some of the more unscrupulous ones. She had known some wonderful men in her life—her father, Ki, Deputy Marshal Long in Denver. It was seldom that she met a man who measured up to them. In fact, she never expected to meet one. So it was a special pleasure to find a young man like Deighton, who seemed, on the surface at least, to possess the qualities she admired in a man.

They arrived shortly at the Savoy Grill. It was a small but elegant place attached to the hotel at the corner of Twelfth and Baltimore Streets. They were greeted by a white-jacketed captain as they descended a short staircase into the restaurant. The captain said, "Good evening, Mr. Deighton," and glanced Jessie's way with a friendly nod.

"Do you have a table in a corner, Armstrong?" Deighton said.

"Yes, sir. This way, please." Armstrong led the couple to a table far from the door, in a semi-dark, intimate corner of the place.

"Thank you," Deighton acknowledged, helping Jessie into her chair. He sat opposite her and asked, "Do you like it?"

Looking around the room at the beautifully appointed tables and well-dressed people who were dining there, she said, "So far, so good. I assume the food lives up to its promise."

"It does," he said. He signaled for a waiter and ordered a bottle of wine. While waiting for the wine, he shifted somewhat uncomfortably in his chair.

Jessie was at a loss for words herself. She sat almost primly, waiting for the young man to say what was on his mind. She wanted to laugh, but held herself back. Could it be that she had tied his tongue?

Finally she said, "I hope you're going to tell me about yourself and your business. I'd like to know who I might be selling my herd to."

Deighton's lips curved into a wry smile. "I'm not a very good talker. But I'll try."

"They say talk is cheap, and it's true. But people can't get to know much about each other unless they talk."

"I've certainly heard of you—of the Circle Star, that is," Deighton said. "Your father had a big name in these parts for many years. I hear that he was killed some time ago. I'm sorry. In fact, my dad knew him. Perhaps Mr. Starbuck mentioned him—Philip Deighton."

"I don't recall," Jessie said. "Is your father still involved in the business?"

A cloud passed over the young man's face. "Not really. Not very much, anyhow. He's . . . well, retired now. I'm carrying most of the load these days. He had more than his share of bad luck."

Deighton fell silent for a moment, and the waiter returned with the wine. Tasting it, nodding his approval, Deighton took the bottle and poured a glassful for Jessie, then filled his own glass.

She offered a toast. "To our fathers. Good men."

"And to us," Deighton added. "For a profitable transaction."

"Very good wine," said Jessie as the fragrant liquid slid down her throat. The waiter lighted a tall red candle on their table. The wine, the cozy atmosphere of the place, her companion's dark brown eyes—all made her warm. She pressed him to continue. "What happened to your father?" she asked.

He took another long drink of wine, then said, "My dad was here before Kansas City even existed as such. Westport Landing, south of here, was the place where all the traders came, and the steamboats. It was a wild town then. All kinds of people—families going west, drunks and saloonkeepers, Mormons, missionaries, Negro freedmen, Chinese, Mexicans, some rough characters of no particular profession, gamblers, riverboatmen, soldiers . . .

"Dad used to say those were the best times—before everything settled down and all the colorful folks moved out. That's not to say Kansas City is a dull place. We have our share of wild times. Just the other day, before you came, a fellow was shot dead—backshot by a jealous husband. Only trouble was, the husband shot the wrong man. Now the husband is in the city jail, awaiting trial. And the wife has moved in with her lover.

"The place is small enough so everybody knows everybody else's business, but big enough to draw people from the outside to do business—business of all kinds. Men like my father have made Kansas City a big cow town, the best thing that ever happened here, most likely. He started a meat-packing operation twenty years ago, then expanded into all areas of the cattle business—investing in ranches up north, outside of St. Joe, stockyards, even refrigerated railroad cars, the coming thing. But he was too successful. Made too many enemies."

Deighton paused. Jessie watched him as he spoke. He became animated when describing how his town had grown over the years, what part his father had played in that growth. But something had happened to his father.

"What do you mean, too many enemies?" she asked.

The young man shrugged, sipping his wine. "You, of all people, should know what I mean. Isn't that what happened to your dad? Only mine is still alive, thank God. If they had their way, though, both of us would be out of business. I'm carrying on for him. I owe it to him."

"Who are his enemies?"

"Hard to tell at any given time. But one I know for sure—always has been and always will be my father's chief opponent in this town: Jason Weatherby, the president of the United National Bank, biggest in town. You ever heard of him?"

Jessie swallowed hard. "Yes. I met him just this morning."

"Well, if I was you, I'd steer clear of that son of a—Sorry, Miss Starbuck."

"What did he do to your father?"

"It's a long story." His face drawn, his voice hard, he continued, "Weatherby knows a good thing when he sees it—and he'll want a piece of it. Ten or twelve years ago he was new in town, just working his way up in the bank, when he first met my father, who had done business with United National for a long time. Weatherby wormed his way into control over Dad's account. I don't know how he did it. But pretty soon Weatherby was calling the shots, preventing Dad from moving quickly when he wanted to buy into some operation, or urging him to invest in Weatherby's friends. Dad thinks he didn't act alone—that somebody else was pulling Weatherby's strings. That I don't know, either."

An edge of sorrow entered his voice as he went on. "Dad's problem is that he's a fighter. He fought Weatherby, withdrew his account from the bank and put it elsewhere. But by that time Weatherby was moving up rapidly in the bank, and six years ago he was made president. He made a lot of powerful friends here, and used them. He'll use anybody if it'll make him some money or win him a fight. So he moved against Dad. Suddenly the other cattlemen stopped dealing with us—our yards were empty and we had no meat to pack and sell. My father's so-called friends stopped spending time with him, avoided him in public. That hurt him bad. My mother died when I was ten, and he depended on his friends for company. I don't know what Weatherby has, but he must have something on every businessman in Kansas City, the way they kowtow to him."

Jessie said, "You're still in business. What happened?"

"Very simple—Dad had a heart attack two years ago. He was weakened by it. He blamed it on Weatherby—but he couldn't do anything about it. The doctor told him to stop working so hard or he'd die. He wanted to go back to work, but I told him the same thing, told him I didn't want him to die. So, as I said, he's pretty much retired now. Bitter as hell about the whole thing. And—strange—Weatherby hasn't bothered me a bit since I took over. Business is better, and some of Dad's old friends have said they're sorry. They come to visit him once in a while. He's glad to see them, but he can't trust them anymore, not after what they did. He can't forget."

"I don't blame him," Jessie sympathized. "And at least you still have him."

"Yeah, I'm glad about that," said Deighton. "He's been real good to me, raising me without a mother. He sent me away to college for two years to fancy me up some. And he made sure that I won't die a poor man."

"He sounds a lot like my father," Jessie mused. Deighton refilled their wine glasses and she took another sip. It was cool and tasted fine. "I guess we've both been lucky to have such men to look up to."

"But I fear for his life. He's not healthy and he still holds a hard grudge against Weatherby. It eats away at him."

"I don't like what I hear about Weatherby. I told you I met him today. He was a real cold fish, but he seemed to know what he was doing, all right," she said.

"Oh, when it comes to money, nobody knows more about it than Jason Weatherby," Deighton concurred. "Just don't believe a word he says or trust him farther than you can throw him. He's out for himself, and only himself. He'll have your throat slit as soon as say good morning to you."

"Aren't you exaggerating some, Mr. Deighton?"

"About him slitting throats? Not much. It's never been proved, but some folks believe that Weatherby has had men killed in his day. Of course, he's too smart to get his own hands bloodied. But they say he has friends in the killing business. His bank's never been robbed; there's never even been an attempt. Some think that's because he has the tightest security; others think he throws enough business in the way of out-of-town criminals that they don't need to rob him."

"Do you have any proof of this?" Jessie asked, not quite ready to accept the magnitude of these charges. "Have you gone to the law?"

Deighton sighed. "No, on both counts. He's just too damned slick. No way to catch him. Besides, the law here is not inclined to cross Jason Weatherby—he lines too many pockets in the police department and in the city council. That's the way he is."

"I just don't see how one man could have such a hold on a whole town," said Jessie. "Why is everybody so scared of him?"

"I'm not scared of him. I hate his guts," the young man spat. "I don't care what the others do. I'm not going to wind up like my father, sick and eaten away from inside. I've promised myself to make Jason Weatherby crawl before I'm done with him. He'll pay for what he did."

To Jessie, Deighton's vow sounded very much like the one she herself had taken after Alex Starbuck's death. She could understand the debt he felt he owed the man who had given him life. Her devotion to her own father's memory was equally strong.

Deighton ordered dinner for both of them, and they drank more wine. Jessie was careful not to become lightheaded, but she enjoyed drinking the delicious vintage. As they waited for their meal, he asked her to tell him about her life.

"It's unusual to see a woman doing what you're doing," he said, with admiration in his voice.

Jessie realized that this was so. She told him about growing up at the Circle Star and learning to ride like a boy and acting very little like a girl. She had always loved the outdoors, and when the old Japanese housekeeper and nurse, Myobu, had tried to keep her inside to learn the feminine arts, Jessie had rebelled. She laughed now as she described her childhood to this friendly young man.

"I was a spoiled little tomboy, but I knew that my father loved me. I didn't have everything I wanted—no little girl ever does—but I had horses and Myobu and Ki and him. He used to tell me, as I got bigger, that I was very much like my mother, and he was proud of me." Jessie told Deighton how her mother had died, in a suspicious accident overseas, how Alex Starbuck had never really stopped grieving for the beautiful woman he had loved.

"I barely remember her," said Jessie. "But from talking with my father, I know everything about her."

"She must have been quite a woman," Deighton said.

They ate their meal, a delicious dinner of catfish that was as thick and tasty as a sirloin steak. The waiter hovered near their table to fill their glasses and remove their plates when they had finished. They had consumed two bottles of wine and declined a third, asking for coffee instead. While they drank the coffee, Deighton asked her whether she minded if he smoked.

"No," she assured him. "I've never enjoyed smoking, myself, but I know how men do."

As he took out a slim cigar and lit it from the candle on the table, he looked at her with an eyebrow cocked. "You have smoked?"

She smiled, her teeth gleaming in the candlelight, a hand to her breast. "In secret, of course. Behind the shed when nobody was looking."

Deighton laughed, a full-throated laugh from deep in his heart. "I can't picture it. The pretty redheaded girl behind the shed acting like a tough boy. I wish I'd been there to see you." His level gaze settled on her face.

"I was pretty naughty as a child," she said, the wine and the warmth of the restaurant bringing a slight flush to her cheeks.

He drained his coffee and sat back in the comfortable chair. "I can imagine," he said.

Outside, it was colder. They had spent over two hours at the Savoy Grill, and the issue of Deighton's bid for Jessie's herd had not come up. She pulled her shawl more tightly around her shoulders and said, "We didn't even talk about business."

Deighton said, "We have tomorrow to talk. I better not make an offer with all that wine in my belly. Makes a fellow a bit unhinged, the wine. You might take advantage of me."

Jessie stopped. They were near a streetlamp, and very few people were out at this hour. The bracing air counteracted some of the effects of the wine. Deighton stood near her. He was so tall that he obscured the gaslight, his shoulders so broad that he looked as if he had been carved out of the side of a mountain.

She said, "I'd never take advantage of you, Patrick." And she meant it.

"I know you wouldn't, Jessie."

It was the first time they had each spoken the other's given name. It was as if they had crossed some unseen territorial border.

Deighton took Jessie's arm and they walked another few blocks in silence. The silence, however, was not a heavy one; instead, it was a tender, unspoken communication. Beneath the black, star-glittering sky, they were drawing irresistably closer.

Again they stopped, this time in a darkened passageway between two buildings. And this time Deighton took Jessie in his arms and brought her to him. She yielded, lifting her lips to his, and they kissed. She felt his breath mingle with her own as her breasts pressed against his solid torso. His arms enveloped her and she lifted hers around him. For a blinding minute they kissed, hard. Deighton then cradled her head, his fingers entwined with her lovely hair. They parted for a moment but came together again, unable to deny the mandate of their feelings.

After a while Jessie said, "You'd better take me back to my hotel. It's getting colder out here."

"All right," Deighton agreed. "I don't want you to freeze."

"Patrick, do you know what you're doing?" she asked him frankly.

"Not really," he admitted. "All I know is that you're the prettiest filly I've ever known, Jessie, and I want to know you a lot better."

"I wish—I wish we had more time," she sighed. She lay her head lightly against his arm. "I don't usually . . . that is, we don't know each other very well yet, Patrick."

They arrived at the front door of Jessie's hotel. The light

from the lobby spilled out onto the sidewalk, casting their tall shadows into the street. Deighton did not let go of her arm.

She said, "Are you going to let me go to my room?"

Deighton said, "No. Not if I don't have to. Jessie, I—"

"We both have much to do tomorrow. I need my sleep, and you need yours."

Although Deighton was a city-dweller, he had the frontier in his blood and that made him somewhat reckless. "I'll see you to your door," he offered.

Jessie read the look on his face: Deighton wanted her. She had to make a choice. She wanted him, too, but if they were to conduct business properly, it might not be the best thing. When she had to be, Jessie was all business. Tonight, however, she felt more like a woman. It was nothing she had control over; it was simply a fact of life.

"Yes," she said. "I'd like that." She led him into the lobby and up the carpeted stairs. She could not hear their footfalls, only her own heart beating.

The young man held on to her arm, striding with long legs beside her. She had given him the key, and when they stopped at her door he put it into the keyhole and unlocked the door. Jessie opened it and stepped inside.

"I can order up some brandy, if you'd like."

"Yes, I would like that," he replied.

With a sash pull, she summoned a porter and told him to fetch a bottle. Closing the door, she turned to Deighton. "Have a seat," she invited, indicating the sofa against the far wall. She joined him there.

A desperate surge of fear and anticipation ran through Jessie as she sat so close to Deighton. She could hear her own breathing above his, feel her heart pounding wildly.

Deighton leaned over, taking her shoulders in his large hands, and kissed her. His hands tightened around her, and she did not resist the strong pull, lifting her face to his. Jessie allowed it to happen, knowing it was irresistable—

knowing that she did not want to stop this strange but friendly man whom she trusted instinctively.

Jessie slipped her arms through Deighton's, clutching him to her. She ran her hands up and down his broad, well-muscled back, feeling the bull-like strength there, pulling him closer. Together in a powerful embrace, they kissed long and lovingly, his tongue darting between her moist lips, exploring the depths of her open mouth. Hungrily, Jessie pushed her own tongue against his, eager to taste him.

A knock at the door forced them apart. Jessie answered the door and came back with a bottle of brandy and two glasses on a lacquered tray. She put the tray on a small table that sat near the couch. "I'm not very thirsty right now," she said huskily.

"I am—but not for brandy, Jessie," Deighton replied.

She came back to him, into his arms. The room was illuminated only by a lamp near her bed. Outside, it was only darkness. But they saw only each other, and they kissed again, tasting, drinking in not brandy but the love between a man and a woman.

Sitting close against him, looking up into his eyes, Jessie fingered Deighton's tie, tugging at it. He helped her untie it, then she began to unbutton his shirt—until finally it fell open and she ran her hand over his chest. It was hard and matted with soft dark hair, ridged with muscle. Her fingers lingered over his dark nipples, teasing him. Then she bent and took one of the nipples between her teeth and bit lightly. He shivered and pushed her away.

"Damn, woman," he breathed. "What are you trying to do?"

"Just to make you feel good," she replied, caressing his chest.

As if in answer, his hands began to move over her body, gently but with a determination to discover every soft curve she possessed.

Jessie reached to unfasten her own blouse, allowing it to slip from her shoulders. As she did, her breasts fell free and open to his touch. She saw his eyes glow and heard him catch his breath as he touched them, felt their perfect roundness. His hands sent wonderful sensations through her, up and down her spine, as he caressed the soft globes and brushed over his distended nipples with his rough fingers. She thrust her shoulders back and closed her eyes to savor the agonizingly sweet feeling.

Deighton then bent his head down and flicked his tongue first over one nipple and then the other, repaying her earlier teasing with some of his own. Nibbling and lightly sucking there, he succeeded in arousing this beautiful young woman as she had not been aroused in a long time.

Meanwhile, Jessie ran her fingers through his curly brown hair, tracing the curve of his head, holding him there at her breasts. Her breathing became irregular as every touch of teeth and tongue sent hot bolts through her body. She closed her eyes tight, gritting her teeth, and took another deep breath before pulling him away.

"God, Patrick . . . what you're doing to me . . ." She could not even put it in words, but kissed his forehead.

"Jessie, let's go to your bed. I want—I want to do it proper," he said.

They stood. A deeper urgency grew within her, and Jessie lifted her face to his to kiss him once more. Deighton's moist lips burned against hers as she pulled his shirt completely off and threw it aside. She then reached for his belt as he began to undress her, too. Within a few seconds they were both naked, and they went to the bed together.

She blew out the lamp, and now the soft blue light from the night sky shafted into the room from the window.

"Come, Jessie," he said to her, easing her down beside him on the soft bed.

Once again she explored the length of his hard body. This time she reached for and found his tumescent length.

It filled her grasp, and Jessie let out a gasp of delight as she discovered its size. She wrapped her fingers around his manhood and pumped it gently, feeling it stiffen in her hand.

Deighton took a gulp of air. "Damn, you've got a strong grip, gal."

"I'm not going to squeeze too hard," she reassured him. "Besides, I don't think I could hurt you. You're made of steel, Patrick," she teased.

She flicked her thumb over the knoblike tip of his organ, feeling a drop of moisture there. Her mind reeled as she imagined this shaft inside her, and she felt her own wetness between her legs.

Deighton, as he nuzzled her neck, kissing her there hotly, slid his own hand down between her silky legs, reaching for the soft patch of hair there. With one extended finger he probed her wet nether lips; finding the fragrant secret chamber that glistened with moist desire, he slowly inserted that finger. It was tight, but he gently pushed his way in.

Closing her eyes, Jessie gasped. It had been all too long since she had had a man—especially one as desirable as Patrick Deighton. She wanted him so badly she could not express it. Now, as she felt him penetrate her with the daring finger, she wanted it all. He worked around and around, slowly, to prepare her for what was to come.

Continuing to arouse her in this way, with his thumb he located the sensitive button above the snug, sweet channel of her love and gently rubbed it, causing Jessie to cry out again as a shock of pleasure shot up her spine. She clutched him tighter, her fingernails scratching his naked back.

He manipulated her with slightly increasing speed, rubbing her there and inserting his finger deeper inside her. She moved her hips to match his teasing fingers, stifling the cries that she felt welling up within her.

Then, suddenly, Campbell withdrew his hand and pulled her to him, crushing her breasts against his strong chest. His insistent, blood-engorged sword stood between them.

He kissed her face and jawline and neck, lingering there, brushing his lips hotly against her warm skin.

"I've got to have you, Jessie," he said in a husky tone.

"Yes," she whispered. "Patrick, please take me . . . please do it . . . now."

Jessie guided his stiff, throbbing shaft to the sweet, inviting channel, helping him to enter her. A dart of stabbing pain quickly turned into a deep thrust of pleasure. Suddenly he was inside her to the hilt—and Jessie felt as if she were being impaled to the earth by an unrelenting opponent in battle.

Deighton lifted himself up to hover above her, his hands planted outside her shoulders. Jessie then raised her legs and locked them around the small of his back, giving him better access to her core. Like an untamed stallion, he made love to her. His strokes were long and quick, and she lifted her hips to meet him, matching his wild rhythm with movements of her own.

She closed her eyes and allowed her mind to fly outside her body. This man was giving just as much as he was taking, and she loved it. With Deighton she could soar into the clouds of this dark, cold night, toward the moon and beyond, to the stars. Never had she felt so free, so unshackled by any earthly concerns, as she felt with this man.

Opening her eyes, she saw Deighton's handsome face above her. A strong current of pleasure flashed through her body, and she returned to earth. Jessie felt herself bucking urgently, meeting his savage thrusts, savoring the near agony of his animal-like penetration.

Patrick Deighton clenched his teeth as he rode her, plunging again and again into her. His eyes were locked upon hers; even in the darkness of the room he could see her bright emerald eyes. For a quick moment he pulled out of her almost completely—right to the tip. Then he thrust in again, more deeply than before. His breath was raggedly washing from his lungs.

She writhed beneath him, taking every inch he had to give, wanting more, unable any longer to control her overwhelming desire. It was so sweet, so wild; if he stopped, she knew she would die.

Both of them now were near the brink. Jessie smelled the saltiness of his sweat and tasted the insistence of his tongue as they kissed. Even as she knew she wanted more, she also felt her impending climax as he increased his pace.

She lifted her legs into the air. Deighton rode harder, giving all he had. She matched his strokes, anticipating his orgasm. Then, suddenly, her own climax washed over her body, sending shudders from head to toe. "Oh God—yes!" she cried. "Patrick, come with me—please—oh!"

Deighton himself could hold out no longer. He made a deep, desperate, final thrust into her velvety sheath. His manhood remained stiff even as he released every drop of his passion inside Jessie. He groaned, his eyes clamped shut, his arms around her shoulders. Gradually his strokes became slower and slower, until finally he ceased.

Later, when they both had regained their equilibrium, they lay side by side in the darkness, the bedclothes pulled up snugly. Deighton turned to her again and kissed her gently, his hand touching her chin.

"What is it?" she asked, sensing that something was on his mind.

"I just don't want to see you involved with that Jason Weatherby," he said frankly. "I deal with Roger Penland at the Guarantee Trust. He's a fine man, an honest man. Weatherby is neither."

"I know you're right, Patrick, but—well, something tells me to keep close watch on Weatherby. And besides, my father did business with him years ago."

"Your father never lived in Kansas City. Neither have you. You don't know the man as I do. If anything should happen to you—"

She stroked his hair. "Nothing is going to happen to me.

Nothing except what happened tonight. And that's all your fault."

"That's a damn lie and you know it," Deighton said.

Jessie kissed him long and hard. "Well, maybe you're right," she conceded.

★

Chapter 5

Jessie decided she had little to lose by stirring things up a bit. At breakfast in the hotel dining room, she told Ki, "I'm going to take Patrick's advice and see his banker. I'm not so sure I want to take my money to Weatherby."

Ki said, "Be careful, Jessie. Weatherby is not to be trusted. We don't know what will happen if we cross him."

"That's what Patrick says. There's only one way to find out," she said.

Then Ki told her of his encounter with the servant girl, Heidi, tactfully omitting some of the more interesting aspects. "She seemed frightened. The priest we saw at Weatherby's is with the royal party." He described for Jessie everything the girl had told him about the prince and his entourage. "The priest is the one to watch out for," he concluded.

Jessie said, "Why don't you keep an eye on him, Ki? Find out what he is up to, where he goes, who he sees."

The samurai agreed. "We know he has seen Weatherby, at least."

"I'd like to meet this Prince Klaus fellow, too. The servant girl said he was from Germany? That doesn't inspire confidence." She did not see any direct connection between her being in Kansas City and the prince's entourage being here at the same time, but it was a disturbing coincidence nonetheless. She wondered, too, what game Weatherby was playing. "This is the important out-of-town client Weatherby is spending his time with. But what exactly is the reason he's here?"

"I didn't get from Heidi any idea of just what business the prince has with the bank," Ki went on. "It seems the priest serves as the go-between, perhaps the primary mover . . ." he did not finish his thought. "There's little use in talking about it until we know. I must find out what I can."

"Well, let's see Mr. Penland at the Guarantee Trust and listen to what he has to say. He might come up with a solid offer to put Weatherby out in the cold."

"You know what happens when a wolf is cold and hungry," Ki suggested.

"Yes," replied Jessie. "But in this case it is the wolf's own fault. And if he strikes back, he'll get only what he's asking for."

Ki rose. "When we're finished at the bank, I'll go over to the prince's hotel and see what I can find out."

Jessie put on her hat. "I thought it would be so simple—sell my beef and get back to the ranch. Things never work out so simply anymore, though."

• • •

Jessie returned to the Hotel President at noon. It had been a good meeting with Penland, the president of the Guarantee Trust Company. He had promised to consider her proposal and to respond within twenty-four hours with his decision—and possibly with suggestions on where to put her money. Kansas City, he had said, was ripe for new investments; she was wise, he thought, to come here at this time—especially with money to spend.

That was what she had wanted to hear, and it confirmed in her mind her suspicion that Weatherby was playing games with her.

Ki had gone about finding out what he could concerning the priest, Father Patetta. She hoped that he wouldn't encounter any danger, but in her heart she had the strong feeling that before she left Kansas City, there would be an eruption of some kind.

At the hotel desk, the clerk stopped her. "Letter, ma'am," he said, handing her a white envelope.

In her room, she opened it and read the note inside. It was handwritten on the United National Bank's heavy bond letterhead, and it puzzled her, to say the least.

Dear Miss Starbuck,

On behalf of Prince Klaus von Stumpf of Bavaria, I should like to invite you to dine with his party this evening at eight o'clock at my home on Wornall Road. His Royal Highness would be pleased to make your acquaintance, and Her Royal Highness, the Princess Therese, joins the Prince in requesting your presence.

Your servant,
Jason Weatherby

Jessie had faced duplicity and deceit before in her extensive travels throughout the West. Always somebody wanted something from her—and rarely, if the wanting was strong, did that somebody avoid violence to achieve his ends. She had seen it too many times, perhaps, for her to trust men very easily. She had been shot at too often, attacked or threatened too frequently, lied to so many times that she now usually expected the worst.

This letter from Weatherby rang just such a false note.

Of course, she would attend. An invitation to see the inside of the lair—even an invitation from the wolf himself—was an unavoidable temptation. Besides, why did the prince and his lady want to meet her? Probably Weatherby had told them about her—but *what* had he told them?

Then it occurred to her—she would bring an ally into the enemy's lair. She took up a pen and wrote to Weatherby that she would be pleased to dine with the prince's party tonight, and that she would be pleased to be accompanied by Mr. Patrick Deighton!

The rest of the day was uneventful. Jessie spent a little while consulting her copy of her father's detailed diary to see if there was any mention at all of the prince or the priest—or even of Weatherby. There were none.

She rehearsed in her mind the genesis of the trip, the railroad trip which had turned into a violent event in itself, her meeting with Weatherby, her affair with Deighton, and now, tonight . . . and it didn't add up right. Having set out for Kansas City with one purpose, she was being confronted with a different result from the one she had anticipated.

When, for the second night in a row, Patrick Deighton came for her, she was in a strangely venomous mood. The first thing she said to him was, "So what are you going to offer me for my beef? You've had time to think it over."

Deighton, sensing that this volatile young lady had a lot on her mind, said, "I'll pay seventy-five dollars a head."

"That's ridiculously low," she said, taking his arm and looking straight ahead. "I had planned on accepting no less than twice that amount—one hundred fifty dollars a head."

"Plans often don't work out." He helped her into a carriage. "We can talk more about it if you'd like."

"I'm sick of talk," Jessie said when the carriage got under way, Deighton sitting beside her in the plush seat. "Ever since I got here, all that's happened is talk. And tonight more talk. Fancy dinners and"—she gestured at her immediate surroundings—"fancy carriages. What does it all add up to? What do people do here besides talk?"

"Jessie," Deighton said, "you're not being fair. I just offered you a good price for your herd. We can bargain, reach a better price, there's no harm in that. I think you have run into the worst this town has to offer, in the person of Weatherby. If you can get past him to the real people of this town, you'll see that it's a good place here."

Jessie tossed her head, the gesture Deighton so liked. "All right, maybe I'm flying off the handle. But, damn it, what does Weatherby want from me? If the man would come right out and say it, I could tell him what I think of him. Oh, Patrick, I'm not making any sense, because I'm angry."

She was used to results. On the ranch she directed the entire operation, and the foreman reported to her and she made the decisions. But here she was asking someone else, this white-collared banker, to make a decision. She wished Patrick Deighton were the banker.

"That's probably exactly what he wants, Jessie. Don't lose your temper with him. Leave that to me—because he can't hurt me anymore. Hell, I was planning on being on my best behavior tonight, and look at you—spitting nails like a blacksmith already."

Finally, Jessie had to smile. "I can't help it, Patrick. When I get angry, I have to let somebody know I'm angry. I don't like being used by men like Weatherby. Too many have tried. It makes me sick."

Jason Weatherby's house was a rambling, two-story stone structure on a large, tree-covered estate, away from the heart of the city. Tonight, in anticipation of the festivities, it was brightly lit, the windows glowing golden against the dark, dense night. A black servant greeted Jessie and Deighton at the front door and escorted them inside.

A grand foyer led to a vast sitting room where the other guests were assembled. Jessie stiffened; she did not like being among a roomful of people, though she was often in such situations. Loving the outdoors and the open sky and the rhythm of a horse, she was not a social creature. She had learned, however, to handle herself well at such times. And she gathered herself, posture erect, for the job at hand.

Weatherby, his iron-gray hair and whiskers stiff and perfumed, greeted Jessie animatedly and gave Deighton's hand a brisk, formal shake. "I have not seen you in years, Deighton."

"Oh, you've seen me, Mr. Weatherby, you've just never spoken to me," the younger man stated.

"I see," Weatherby said. "We'll have to rectify that situation, won't we?"

"Not necessarily," said Deighton.

"Please, Miss Starbuck, come and meet the others. This is the first time I have ever entertained European royalty in my house." Weatherby took Jessie from Deighton and led her across the carpeted room. Overhead, a massive chandelier hung from the vaulted ceiling.

"His Royal Highness Prince Klaus," Weatherby intoned, gesturing toward a very tall man, resplendent in a blue and pink and gold uniform, with a violet sash across his chest. "Miss Jessica Starbuck," he said, guiding Jessie toward the prince.

Jessie took the prince's large, soft hand. "I am pleased to meet you, Prince Klaus." She did not curtsy with excessive formality. She met the prince on his own terms, gripping his hand firmly.

The prince, on the other hand, inclined his head and clicked his heels together in a snappy salute. "My dear Miss Starbuck, I have heard so much about you from Mr. Weatherby. I am so happy to make your acquaintance." His English was impeccable.

She guessed the prince to be in his early forties. He had that stance which she imagined a prince should have: shoulders thrust back, spine ramrod-straight, booted legs together. The severely noble cut of his chin was somewhat overshadowed by his big, almost pouting pink lips, visible beneath a bushy mustache of a sandy hue, the same color as his hair, which was brushed back from his forehead. She detected the unmistakable scent of rosewater about him, and talcum powder. A giant rock—a diamond, it looked like—glittered on his left ring finger, and medals flashed on his breast—medals from wars he couldn't have fought, Jessie told herself.

He said, "I should like to present my wife, Princess Therese. *Liebchen,* this is Miss Jessica Starbuck of Texas." Prince Klaus practically lifted Therese's hand so that Jessie could touch it.

"Pleased to meet you," Jessie said.

The princess was like a porcelain doll, small, all white and shiny and clothed in beautiful satin and lace. Her round, angelic face was dominated by two big gray eyes; her nose was upturned above two rose-red lips and a smooth chin. Jessie saw little intelligence but a lot of innocent faith in those eyes.

Weatherby stepped in, smiling conspiratorily. "And you must meet Father Albino Patetta, the prince's confessor and advisor."

Jessie turned to confront the priest face to face for the first time. Yes, he was the man she had seen at the bank yesterday. The long black soutane seemed to envelop him—except for his head. Without the biretta, she could see that his black hair was thinning on top. The heavy, bushy eyebrows moved up and down as he spoke. *"Buona sera,* Miss Starbuck. We did not have the opportunity to meet at Signor

Weatherby's office. I regret that oversight now."

In contrast with that of the prince, the priest's hand was work-roughened, callused, and hard, the fingers long, with tufts of hair at the knuckles. Perhaps he had spent his youth in the vineyards of his native country. For whatever reason, he was not unused to physical labor.

"Padre," Jessie acknowledged. She looked into his dark, luminous eyes, trying to read what was behind them, but she could not. All she could sense was an immense, bottomless coldness in him. He wore his robe and his collar and his title of "man of God" the way a wolf wears the proverbial sheep's clothing. It ill-fitted him.

There were other royal retainers and members of the Kansas City social elite whom Jessie met. In all, Weatherby had gathered about two dozen people for this "intimate" evening. Jessie stifled her impatience and, keeping Patrick Deighton close by, sipped on a glass of wine as dinner was being prepared in the seemingly distant kitchen. She watched the priest and Weatherby huddle in one corner for several minutes. And she wondered what, if anything, Ki had found out today. She had not seen Ki since noon.

Turning to Deighton, she asked, "Do you know these people?"

"Most of them," he replied. "I grew up with them, or with their children. They are the pillars of the community, you might say. Awfully upstanding people. Churchgoers, most of them. I'm sure they don't like the sight of a Roman priest in the same room. They like to stick to their own kind."

Jessie was pleased that she was seated next to Prince Klaus at the table. She wondered why Weatherby had allowed her such a privileged position, one that Kansas City society women surely coveted.

"Your country is so beautiful, what I have seen of it," the prince was saying as the first course was served. "I and my wife and children are set to embark upon a trip which will cover much of the Western territories. Perhaps we shall see some of your buffaloes and the red savages, the Indians, which we hear so much about in my country."

"There aren't many buffalo left," Jessie commented. "The white man has wiped out nearly all of them."

Prince Klaus frowned, his entire mustache drooping. "That is a sad story you tell, Miss Starbuck. Were the white men starving that they had to kill so many buffaloes?"

"No," said Jessie. "They did it for the sport."

"Oh, I see." He scratched his mustache. "I had hoped to shoot one myself. I am considered a skilled hunter in my country. That is a sad story," he repeated.

He went on to outline for her—in excruciating detail—the itinerary for their Western journey. She was only half listening. Looking down the table, she saw Deighton trapped between two elderly ladies, obviously pressing him to reveal his plans for marriage or to encourage him to meet a young niece or granddaughter. Directly across from her sat Father Albino Patetta, the priest. She caught him glancing her way more than once. He was deep in conversation with the princess. Jessie saw the priest's eyes fall into the beautiful lady's cleavage a few times too many.

When she could get in a word edgewise, she asked the prince about Patetta.

"The dear father is perhaps my closest friend," Klaus said. "He comes from Rome, where he grew up and was educated. I met him through the archbishop in Cologne, who recommended him highly. Father Patetta has been with me for five years, and what a comfort and a help he is!" The elegantly groomed prince lifted a glass of wine to his lips. Then he said, "Not only in the affairs of the soul, mind you. The man has an uncanny ability to advise me on matters of state and finance as well. He is truly invaluable to me."

Jessie was beginning to get the picture now. Patetta had certainly established a strong position in Prince Klaus's household. He was no mere confessor, but the prince's right-hand man. Invaluable! She could imagine how invaluable he was; a man in Claus's position needed somebody to do his necessary dirty work. What better candidate than a man in a black robe, with the Church to back him up? But, she asked the prince, weren't most of the German nations Protestant?

"Yes they are. They fell away from the true Church in Martin Luther's time. My family, however, kept the faith, through years of hostility and persecution. We have always been loyal to the Holy Roman Empire—in fact, some of my ancestors have been Emperors. Mine is a small state in Bavaria, and we have always been in the midst of political and religious conflicts—for more than eight hundred years." His chest puffed out and the medals rattled. He was certainly a regally, rigidly proud man.

Gently, subtly, she probed deeper. Did Prince Klaus know the leaders of his neighboring nation, Prussia? Jessie hadn't ceased to wonder if the prince was in any way connected with the hated cartel that included so many businessmen and leaders from that part of Europe. Even if his name did not appear in Alex Starbuck's diary...

The prince answered her frankly, guilelessly, but none of the men he named were any of whom she had heard—or read in her father's records—before.

She said, "Do you have business in Kansas City, other than arrangements for your Grand Tour?"

"Yes we do." The second course came and a new bottle of wine was opened. The prince eyed both food and drink appreciatively; clearly, he was a practiced sensualist. "Father Patetta sometimes protects me too efficiently—for my own good, he tells me. I am not certain of the exact nature of our financial interest here, but the good father assures me he is working to increase the family's wealth through prudent investments in Kansas City."

Jessie had never heard such hogwash. Could it be true that this wealthy German prince did not know or care how the priest spread his money around? She doubted it, yet Prince Klaus seemed perfectly aware of what he was saying, and didn't seem to mind the implications of such a course of action.

The priest had, it seemed, his full confidence.

"Pardon my boldness, Your Highness," she said, "but do you trust Father Patetta to control your finances without even consulting you?"

"I do," he answered without pause.

"I admire your faith in your fellow man," she said sardonically.

"Father Patetta is no ordinary man, Miss Starbuck. He is a man of God and a man of keenest intelligence. I would trust him with my life, or with my wife's life, or my children's."

She wanted to have a word with this superman of a priest, and when supper was over she had her chance. Seeing Deighton still tied up between the two women, she was able to maneuver to Patetta's side as the priest continued to talk to Princess Therese.

Upon closer examination, Jessie was even more impressed with the princess's beauty. It was of a delicate sort so uncommon here in the West, bred of a long, unbroken tradition in royal Europe. Probably she could trace her ancestry to some matron in the ancient Roman Empire, so classic were her features, so clear was her skin. She smiled prettily, her gray eyes glittering, when she spoke to the priest. It looked to Jessie as if he had her complete confidence as well as the prince's.

The princess excused herself with an imperial nod to Jessie, and returned to her husband's side. The priest turned to Jessie. "Did you enjoy the meal?" he asked her.

"Yes," she said. She had hardly tasted the rich, well-chosen food or wine, so intent had she been upon learning as much as she could from Prince Klaus. Looking at the priest, she could see that beneath the dark robes he was a trim figure, lean and graceful. Remembering his hands, she wondered anew at what kind of life he had lived before taking his Holy Orders as a Catholic priest.

"The prince tells me you are from Rome," she said.

"Yes. That is where I was born. I lived in many places before returning to study for the priesthood. Rome is the only place I truly consider home."

He spoke with a thick accent, but he knew English well. Presumably he knew German and Latin, too. A smart-as-a-whip young fellow, well traveled, and a wielder of some power in the prince's court. He was not to be underestimated, she reminded herself.

"How do you find life in Germany? It must be very different from Rome."

"Indeed. It is colder, the food is not as rich, and the wine is not as good. But the people, the Catholics, are strong and intelligent and very much committed to their faith. As a servant of the Church, it warms my heart to see their faces. And the prince himself is a wonderful man. He is not pretentious, but he knows that he was born to a high station; there is not a false bone in his body. I consider it an honor to toil at his side."

Jessie changed the subject. Why beat around the bush? she thought. She wanted to see the cleric's reaction to a direct question. "You are very intimately involved in the prince's financial affairs, I understand."

Patetta was unflustered. "Yes, he asked me, as his spiritual advisor, to share my knowledge of worldly commerce."

"When did you have time to acquire such worldly knowledge?" she asked.

The priest's mouth was a grim slash across his face. He did not like her question. "It is simply a matter of common sense," he demurred, his voice ringing with disinterest. "I would not be wrong to ask you why you, a young woman, are a cattle rancher. It *is* unusual, you must admit."

"Unusual, yes," she said. "But I don't pretend to be anything other than what I am."

The priest raised an eyebrow and said evenly, "What do you mean by that, my child?"

Jessie said, "I am a rancher, pure and simple—nothing else. You are much more than you appear to be. You are not just a priest. And I am not your child, so please do not call me that."

"It is only a form of address. I use it commonly when speaking to the younger members of my flock. I am nothing more than a priest, Miss Starbuck. I only serve God, and the prince."

She had to admire his stubbornness, if nothing else. "Well, you have been spending more time with Jason Weatherby than I have," she pointed out. "I can't seem to catch his attention."

"Oh, you have captured his attention, Miss Starbuck," Father Patetta said. "He told me he wished he could have spoken with you at greater length. He will, after all, be seeing you tomorrow."

"Are you Weatherby's confessor, too?" she challenged him.

This time the priest laughed. "You are skeptical. That is good, perhaps. Too much doubt, however, can be the work of Satan. The Apostle Thomas learned that from Christ. It would please me much to be able to teach that simple lesson to a woman like you."

The more he spoke, the less pronounced his accent became, until he was talking quite comfortably to Jessie. He was fencing with her, really—with words. She thought, too, that she detected an element of seduction in his words. Ki, she remembered, had told her about the young servant girl who had some bitter words for the priest's behavior.

"How much longer before the prince begins his tour?" she asked, wanting to conclude this particular conversation.

"Two days more," the priest said. "Then we set out for Abilene, in the state of Kansas. Have you ever been there?"

"Yes," said Jessie. "It's not a pretty town."

"But it is a *real* Western town. That is what the prince has been told. That is what he wishes to see."

Luckily, Deighton had extricated himself and now came over to her. She said to Father Patetta, "Excuse me, I must be going. I shall see you again, I'm sure."

The priest bowed gallantly, ignoring Deighton. "God go with you."

"What a goddamned phony," the young cattleman said to Jessie when they were at the door. "All of Weatherby's crowd are like that. Makes me sick to my stomach."

Jessie had an uncomfortable feeling in *her* stomach, a bad taste in her mouth—even after all the good food. "Nothing about Weatherby or this priest rings true. Prince Klaus, I think, is all right. If anything, he's probably being used by the two of them."

Deighton agreed. "Weatherby kept an eye on me all night. Afraid I might embarrass him by talking about my father, I suppose."

"He put you in safe company," she kidded.

"If those two old ladies have anything to say about it, I'll be married within a week."

"I hope not," said Jessie.

The carriage was waiting for them. On the ride to town Deighton kissed her. She responded hungrily, remembering last night.

Too soon, they were back at the Hotel President. Deighton helped Jessie down. And as he turned with her to enter the hotel lobby, a man came running up to him.

"Mr. Deighton!" he called, out of breath.

Deighton stopped. "What is it, Fletcher?"

"Down at the railroad yard, Mr. Deighton—they stampeded the steers. They tore down some of the corrals. It's a mess down there!"

"Jesus Christ," Deighton muttered. "Jessie, I've got to go see what happened."

"I'll go, too. First I better change clothes."

"I don't have time to wait for you," he said, on edge.

"Then go ahead, I'll meet you there. Those are probably some of my cows, too."

She rushed upstairs to her room. Ki was not around. She wondered where he was, and wouldn't be surprised if she met him at the railroad yard. As quickly as she could, she changed into denim trousers and boots, pulling on a dark cotton shirt and her vest.

When she arrived upon the scene nearly a half hour later, all was pandemonium at the railroad yards.

Deighton was sitting horseback, upon a tall, spirited stallion, trying to herd stray cattle into the holding pens. Several other hands were helping, but it was a dirty, difficult job. From where she stood, Jessie could see that six or eight corrals had been smashed open—it looked as thought axes had been used to chop the cows free. Then, she surmised, somebody had stampeded the cattle, causing them to run wild throughout the railroad yard, some of them straying into town.

As she surveyed the damage, Ki came up to her. "Thought you'd be here," she said. "You heard about the stampede?"

Ki's face was streaked with the dust that billowed up from the earth as the hundreds of animals were rounded up once again. He wiped at it with the back of his hand. He spoke in his customary low, even tone—which was difficult to hear above the bawling of the cattle all around them.

"I was outside the royal family's hotel. I was watching for the girl, Heidi. A man came running down the street, shouting that the cattle were stampeding."

Jessie ran a kerchief over her forehead. The activity stirred up heat, along with the dust. She said, "Did you discover anything of interest?"

"No," Ki replied. "What about you, at the dinner party?"

"I spoke with the prince and with the priest, Father Patetta. The priest is the man we must keep an eye on. Prince Klaus relies upon him almost entirely in financial decisions. Patetta is the prince's liasion with Weatherby. He's a smooth talker, too."

"I'm not surprised to learn that," said Ki.

"If you talk to the girl again, ask her about the priest's schedule. I want to know what he does during the day—where he goes and who he sees."

"That should be easy enough," the samurai said. "She's a smart girl, keeps her eyes open."

Jessie took her place again, one foot on the rail, hoisting herself up so as to see better over the vast yard. She saw Deighton wheeling his big horse to drive a stubborn steer into one of the unbroken pens. The drovers' task was made more troublesome by the debris strewn throughout the yard by the wild cattle.

Finally, after nearly another hour's work, the stray beeves were corraled again. In the morning the men would repair the broken pens, count the cattle, and replace them in the holding pens. It would be a tedious job, delaying the sale of the Circle Star herd.

Deighton spurred his horse over to where Jessie and Ki were standing. He wore a look of disgust on his face. He made an incongruous appearance, sitting astride the stallion, still wearing his evening clothes, now torn and dirty, his big hat on his head. He swung down from his mount.

"I've never seen such a mess," he snorted, whipping off his hat. He tried to brush some of the corral dust off his suit, but it was no use. "Damn!" he spat. "Ruined a perfectly good suit. If I was twenty years younger, my dad would whip me half to death for this. Never seen the like." He shook his head in anger, his face scarlet.

"Your men did a good job of containing the cows," Jessie said encouragingly. "It could have been a lot worse."

"Hell, I had two men down here who were supposed to

be guarding these pens. After I fire them tomorrow, I'll hire them back and double the guard. Whoever did this knew exactly how and when to strike."

"Who do you think did it?" Jessie braced for the expected answer.

"By God, who else?" Deighton raged. "Weatherby and his cronies! I told you they've been after my father for years. Now, with the biggest potential season I've ever had, they're trying to sabotage me. I don't have any doubt who it was."

"But can you prove it, Patrick?" she asked, trying to bring him down to earth.

In her bones she felt Deighton was right, but she knew he needed rock-solid proof if he was going to challenge Weatherby in a court of law. It galled her to think it was possible that the banker would do such an underhanded, destructive act.

"Hell, any trace of the intruders has been wiped away by the stampede and by me and my men, trying to get the steers back in." Deighton put a big hand on Jessie's shoulder. "You know what they say about the needle in the haystack? Well, that's about what it will be like, trying to pin anything definite on Weatherby. He hides his tracks too well. He's a professional."

"He had to hire somebody to do this piece of dirty work for him," Jessie suggested. "If we could somehow find those men, make them talk . . ."

"That is a big 'if,' Jessie," Ki put in. "Even if you both are right. There are many men in Kansas City, many alibis for a man if he needs one."

"Well, see what you can find out anyway, Ki," Jessie asked her companion. "Patrick here is going to heed all the help he can get on this one. And by God, I want to sell my herd before it's stampeded all over creation again!"

Chapter 6

Too tired and frustrated to spend the night with Patrick Deighton, Jessie returned to her own room—alone—to sleep. Ki, meanwhile, lingered at the yards. He watched in the darkness illumined only by scattered torches, as Deighton and his men made a quick, rough count of the bawling animals.

Ki had his job cut out for him, and he did not like it a bit. Confronted with an entire city full of suspects, he had to find out, if he could, who was responsible for the stampede. Where to begin?

Ki was contemplating the possibilities, allowing his highly disciplined mind to sift through various plans of action, when Deighton rode over to where he stood. The tall young man sat his saddle with grace and pride, despite his obvious exhaustion. His fine evening clothes were so dusty as to be unsalvageable.

"You can tell Miss Jessie it looks like we didn't lose a single Circle Star cow. We'll get a more accurate count in the morning, and round up any strays that got by us tonight. Shouldn't be too hard to find a cow wandering the streets of Kansas City. And tell her I'll be willing to cover any losses that might have occurred. My responsibility, really."

"She will be glad to hear that," said Ki. "But I'm sure she will say that you are not responsible. This attack was as much against her as against you."

"She hasn't been in town long enough—" Deighton began, but Ki cut him off.

"Jessie, like her father before her, has many enemies in many places. Some she has never yet met, in places she has never yet been. It is not right that this should be so—but there it is."

"I think I know what you mean, Ki." The rangy young man swung down from his horse, removing his hat and wiping his brow again. It would take a long, hot bath to rid him of the grit and the frustration of this night.

Ki said, "You have enemies, too. Who are they?"

Deighton gave a bitter laugh. "There is one man—one man only—whom I consider my enemy. The only one I care about. Jason Weatherby. That's what I told Jessie. The others—there aren't many—don't count. It's only Wheatherby." He turned and spat disgustedly between two rails.

The samurai tried hard to see the stars in the black vault of the night sky. The dust clouds among the disturbed corrals had not settled, and still obscured his vision. One by one, the men put out the torches they had lit to allow them to work. Beside him, Deighton bulked large in the hazy darkness.

"You and Miss Jessie are sort of strangers in town, but I feel that you're my friends. I'm not one to trust folks very easily." He spoke openly, frankly with Ki, who listened with appreciation. "But with her, it's different. A hell of a lot different. You know what I mean, Ki."

"Yes I do. Jessie and I have been friends for many years."

"Well, you're goddamned lucky—that's all I can say. Will you let me buy you a drink downtown?"

Ki smiled. "Not a bad idea. It would clear this dust from our throats. Also, I sometimes find out more in a saloon then I do in the offices of a town's leading citizens." He smiled.

"Hell, you'd be talking about Weatherby. That tight-assed, mean sonofabitch wouldn't tell his mother the truth. I wouldn't trust him as far as I could spit at him."

Deighton walked his mount through the narrow, twisting path between the crowded pens. Ki walked with him. The animals were getting less noisy; they were tired after all the excitement. Ki's rope-soled slippers whispered in the heavy dust as Patrick Deighton's black boots were covered with that same dust. The big horse moved easily, looming behind the two men.

"You should have seen that fancy Prince Whatsizname tonight, Ki. You would have got a good laugh out of that one. Weatherby parading royalty in his house, putting on all sorts of airs. Jessie fit in, though. She fit in real nice—the prettiest gal there, by far."

"Jessie is the most beautiful woman I know," Ki said simply.

Deighton had no reply for that remark. Instead he said, "I'll take you to a place where a lot of cowboys hang around. Give you an idea of who-all calls Kansas City home away from home. They come from all over the West, but mostly from Texas—like you and Jessie. Some of them don't smell too good, though," he added with a chuckle.

"I'm used to the bathing habits of cowhands," Ki said. Indeed, having lived and worked at the Circle Star for many years, the samurai had endured many a noxious day and night in their company, and had even been on a cattle drive or two. He, of course, had been trained differently; his people, the Japanese, prized cleanliness as one of the chief virtues.

The saloon was only a few minutes away from the smashed holding pens at the railroad yard. Deighton tethered his horse at a short hitch rail in front of the place. Ki had noticed that there were not many such rails in Kansas City—a sign, probably, that the town was getting bigger and more sophisticated.

With Ki behind him, Deighton pushed his way into the saloon. It was dark and smoky inside, the only light coming from four or five gaslamps in various spots around the long room.

Ki estimated that there were at least three dozen men there, most of them crowded near the bar, others at small tables. At two of those tables, card games were in progress. Over all hung a pall of cigar smoke, drifting lazily at nose level for those who were standing. Deighton elbowed his way toward the bar, tossing out greetings to the men he knew. He seemed to know quite a few, and they let him pass easily. When they got a look at Ki, however, their countenances shifted from friendly recognition to suspicion.

Deighton must have seen this, but he gave no clue. He just made sure that Ki was right behind him, and out of harm's way.

Having achieved the lip of the bar, Deighton cleared the way for Ki to join him. The lithe, sure-footed samurai placed himself close to Deighton, but with enough room to maneuver, should it prove necessary. He cast a wary eye around, noting some of the hostile glances he was receiving from the other men. Probably they had never seen a character who looked quite like this half-Japanese, half-American warrior. Ki, in his unconventional slippers and black vest, his crow-black hair falling onto his forehead above his almond-shaped eyes, was an object of curiosity at the very least.

It was a burden Ki carried with him wherever he went in this country. Americans did not trust so-called foreigners, did not like those with other than white skin. That was why they had had slavery in this country, why the Indians were hated and slaughtered, why Mexicans were treated like second-class citizens at best. It was another thing Ki would never understand about his adopted land—why there was so much hatred and suspicion in such a big, open, rich country as the United States. It was something he had to live with as intimately as his own skin.

Deighton ordered a whiskey, and Ki asked for a beer. The bartender brought their drinks. Ki's beer was a bit warm, but tasted good after he'd eaten so much dust earlier. He thanked Deighton.

"My pleasure, Mr. Ki. I needed this myself." He tipped the glass to his lips, draining it.

Deighton then pulled some makings from his coat pocket and proceeded to roll a quirly expertly, with one hand. "Learned to do that from my dad," he said. "Always when I was a button I used to follow him around, imitate his every move. So he taught me how to do this." He put the cigarette between his lips and lit it with a sulfur match. Smoke streamed from his nostrils and he sighed. "Goddamn whoever did that down at the railroad yard."

Ki said quietly, "They might be right here—whoever they are."

The big man ordered another whiskey; Ki still nursed his beer. "Makes me angry," Deighton was saying as he awaited his drink. "Somehow I think Weatherby was involved. Of course, the bastard has a perfect alibi. He was throwing a party at his own house."

"Jessie said that he has contacts among the criminal element around here," Ki put in.

"Yeah, that's how I understand it," said Deighton. He took a swallow of whiskey. "It's never been proved. People who do business with Weatherby don't want to believe it—

at least they don't want to hear about it—as long as they're making money."

"He must be a very rich man," Ki said.

"Rich as Croesus, from what I can tell. But he's still a bastard."

Deighton turned to face Ki directly, bumping into a man who stood at the bar beside him. He paid no attention to the man, who wheeled, his face an angry red. Deighton kept talking to Ki as the man looked from the Oriental to the big cattle buyer.

"What the hell, mister," the man began. "There's room here for everybody."

"Mind your own business," Deighton said out of the side of his mouth. "I'm not talking to you."

"You spilled my drink, mister," the man went on. "You want to buy me a new one?"

"Go to hell," said Deighton.

"Why you sonofa—" The man threw his weight against Deighton, jarring him, causing him to drop his whiskey glass.

Deighton spun around to confront the bothersome man. The stranger was tall and very skinny, unshaven, with pale blue, watery eyes. It was apparent that he was a man who liked his liquor. "Just leave me alone, mister," the bigger man said, trying to defuse the confrontation.

The man would have none of it. He was angry. "Who the hell do you think you are, mister? You don't own this place."

"No, and neither do you, *mister,*" Deighton gritted. "I'll buy you your goddamned drink," he offered.

The man said, "I seen you buy a beer for that slant-eyes over there." He indicated Ki. "I don't drink with China-men." He spat on the sawdust-strewn floor.

Deighton had had enough. He grabbed the front of the man's shirt in his fist and pulled the man toward him, slapping the stranger once, hard, with the back of his ha...

The man opened his mouth to scream, but the impact insured that no sound came out. Instead, blood trickled from his mouth and a tooth fell out. His eyes were afire.

Regaining his senses, the stranger stood his ground, lashing out at Deighton with a left. The big man blocked the punch, delivering a left of his own to the man's gut. The skinny man bent double, the breath whooshing out of his lungs. But he butted Deighton with his head, hitting him right in the groin. Now it was Deighton's turn to wince as pain shot through him.

Watching this, Ki stepped in, trying to pry the two men apart. By now, others at the bar were aroused, some shouting their support of Jimmy—which seemed to be the skinny man's name. The crowd stepped back to give the fighters room. But Ki didn't like this—he knew it was likely these other men would join their friend against Deighton and himself. How to avoid a full-scale brawl? He wasn't sure.

Meanwhile, Deighton had regained his upright position. He raised his arms in a prizefighter's stance, legs apart, fists clenched. He allowed Jimmy to recover before stepping forward. His fists pistoned into the man's face. Jimmy stumbled back. One of his companions caught him, preventing him from falling to the floor. Jimmy shook his head and stood fast. He parried Deighton's blows now, and even sneaked in a quick left that caught the bigger man below the ribcage.

Deighton felt some pain this time. The skinny man was quick—and he was strong. Deighton could not take him for granted. He stepped away from the bar to give himself more room to maneuver, and Jimmy followed him, staying just out of Deighton's reach. Warily the two men circled each other, each having given and taken some hurt, each wanting to dish out some more. Their eyes were locked, their fists ready. Behind and around them, the men in the d closely to witness the fight. Ki, however, rd, waiting for a third party to join the fight— dy to stop that.

lunged, bending low, for Deighton's knees. was able to sidestep the attack, moving lithely for his im ense bulk. He pushed the man's head down, hoping to push him to the floor. He almost succeeded. But Jimmy was quick, too, and he was able to twist free. He jerked up and stood facing Deighton angrily. "Sonofabitch," he muttered.

Deighton ignored the man's words. He was intent only on finishing this fight and getting out of this place in one piece. Like Ki, he knew that at any moment the others might turn from spectators to participants—and he did not want any of that.

He glanced quickly in Ki's direction. The samurai was watching the crowd too, and that reassured Deighton. He turned again to his opponent. Jimmy was burning mad now, ready for some real violence. The skinny man's mouth and chin were a splash of red from Deighton's first blow. Jimmy wiped at the blood with his left hand, snarling.

"Finish him, Jimmy!" one man shouted through the smoky haze of the saloon. Others took up his cry. They did not want to see one of their own beaten.

Deighton concentrated on the skinny man's movements. He moved warily, giving Jimmy wide berth for the moment. As he did, Deighton skirted close to the watching crowd of men. Ready to advance on his opponent, the big man took a step toward him, but felt somebody else's foot hooking his ankle. Too late to sidestep, Deighton fell headlong to the gritty floor. He then felt Jimmy pounce on top of him, pinning him down.

With all his strength—and a large measure of rage—Deighton tried to lift himself up, but the man on top rode him like a bucking bronco. Deighton brought his arms in, attempting to gain some leverage. Finally he did, and with his elbows close in he pushed hard, with all his strength. Jimmy was clutching Deighton's hair, trying to batter the big man's face into the dirty floor. Deighton shook his head and felt the skinny man's hand pull away a fistful of hair.

Blind with anger now, Deighton's face contorted. With a last great effort, he shucked the skinny man off and rolled away. He bolted to his feet and shot a furious glance at the men ringing the two fighters. "I'll take care of you," he muttered, but turned his attention back to the business at hand.

Ki had seen who the culprit was that tripped Deighton. He kept the man—a short, stocky fellow with blond hair and a leather hat—in sight now. He would help Deighton deal with this man, if necessary. Ki could feel the mood of the crowd worsen, turning ugly as Jimmy's supporters saw that their man could not best Deighton. And Ki wondered if he and the young cattleman could handle all these other angry men—with help, perhaps, from a few of Deighton's friends—if they had to.

Meanwhile, through a red mist of rage, Deighton focused on Jimmy's face. Then Jimmy was after him ferociously, aggressively, fists flailing wildly. Deighton raised his guard just in time to shunt fists off his arms and shoulders, bobbing his head to one side so that Jimmy's whistling blow just missed his ear. The skinny man was fast, savage now—making up in swiftness what he lacked in brute strength. Jimmy did not slow down, but kept coming in. His fists kept Deighton rocking back, though they didn't hurt the cattleman.

With the noise of the men a buzz in his spinning head, Deighton watched for his chance. Jimmy grunted and came in again, this time with a strong left that caught Deighton on the chin. Deighton's head snapped back, and Jimmy seized the opening. His right smashed in, chopping Deighton's cheekbone. Before Deighton could recover, the skinny man hit him in the belly.

Desperate, Deighton backed off as best he could, his fists held up in lame defense. The momentum against his opponent had been lost. He had to recover it now. He watched as the skinny man charged in again. This time, Deighton had an idea. He let Jimmy get close, even took another blow in his gut. But he lowered his head and butted it into Jimmy's face, and heard Jimmy gasp. His hair was wet with blood from Jimmy's smashed nose when he jerked his head back. Jimmy howled and backed off for a moment. The crowd in the saloon was eerily silent.

Then somebody called, "Get 'im, Jim! Don't let him hurt you!"

This animated the tall, thin man into action. He ran again at Deighton in a fighting fury, and then it became a real slugging match.

Deighton took punishment and dealt it. The sound of fists on flesh filled the quiet saloon with an ugly, pounding sound as he and Jimmy met blow for blow. Both men were strong, both equally determined. Deighton was bigger, but the skinny man was somewhat quicker. Jimmy got in a blow that rocked Deighton's head, but Deighton gave it back, his knuckles meeting the flesh and bone of Jimmy's face.

In a few minutes both men were nearly exhausted. Panting, they backed off from each other.The bloodthirsty spectators were now buzzing among themselves. Ki even heard one man accept another's side bet on the outcome of the fight. The only thing that reassured Ki was that no one else had jumped in. He looked at Deighton. A cut had opened up under his right eye and it was bleeding now, but he looked unfazed; he was gathering strength while Jimmy seemed to be losing steam. Good, thought Ki, I will get Deighton out of here as soon as it's over.

Deighton ignored the pain and went back in, hard and mercilessly. He took every blow Jimmy gave him, only to return two like it. He connected beneath the skinny man's chin, rocking the head back, and blood sprayed from Jimmy's busted nose. He didn't give the man a second to recover, but stepped forward and delivered a killing gut punch. Jimmy bent double, the air rushing out of him. Deighton lifted him with a powerful right, then went in one more time with his left, landing it soddenly in Jimmy's belly. Jimmy cried out and his knees buckled.

Looking around, his rage yet unspent, his face sprayed with his opponent's blood, Deighton said grimly, "Anybody else want to try? Come on—I'm not going anywhere."

The men murmured among themselves. They had seen one of their own beaten to a bloody pulp, and they did not like it; but which one of them was going to take up Deighton's challenge and risk the same treatment? Two of them stepped forward to drag Jimmy's wrecked body from the scene of the fight. No one else moved.

Deighton returned to the bar and ordered a whiskey. When it came, he drained it in one big gulp. He turned to Ki, who had stood by, ready for anything. "Don't say it. I know I was stupid to fight that jackass. But, hell, I felt like dealing some hurt, and he sure as hell asked for it—you can't say he didn't."

"No," Ki replied. "You wanted to fight. He wanted to fight. Both of you got what you wanted."

Deighton managed a lopsided smile. "Wasn't much fun for you, was it?"

Ki said, "I didn't find out what I wanted to find out. We're no closer to discovering who caused the trouble tonight."

Deighton was a mess. His evening clothes, which had already been soiled beyond repair by the riding down at the railroad yard, were now torn and bloodied from the fight. His face, too, was very much the worse for wear—his lip cut, his hair washed in blood and sweat. He was not very pleasant to look at, and he knew it.

"Sorry. I shouldn't have let that fellow rouse me like he did. Our first job is to find out who's behind the stampede and prove it. I suppose Miss Jessie is all for bringing the case to court. I'd be in favor of punishing the guilty party and leaving it at that."

"Jessie believes that justice is possible in the courts."

"Sometimes it is, sometimes it isn't," Deighton said.

Ki shook his head. "I'll never understand Americans. There is no agreement on what justice really is in this country."

"There never will be—at least not in my lifetime," Deighton mused. "We're too young, too raw to put all our faith in institutions. Some people swear by the law, others can't believe that the law does anything for them. I don't think the law does a damn thing for me."

Jessie had told Ki about Deighton's father, about how Weatherby had nearly ruined the man, and about the son's grudge against the banker. Perhaps, Ki thought, Deighton was right.

Ki said, "It's time to go."

Deighton nodded. "One more drink." He ordered it, drained it, and followed Ki out the door. Both men felt the eyes of the other patrons on them as they left.

The clean, cool air outside was bracing. Deighton breathed deeply. "I've got to clean myself up," he grumbled.

"We'll try again tomorrow," Ki said. "We'll find out who is responsible for this trouble."

Deighton mounted his horse and rode off, leaving Ki to watch him fade into the darkness. Then Ki made his own way back to the hotel.

★

Chapter 7

"Men are such fools sometimes," Jessie said, when Ki told her about the fight Deighton had been involved in. "That's why they need women—to straighten them out."

She and Ki were eating breakfast at the Hotel President, in her room. The sun streamed in, casting a bright glow through the room—in contrast with last night's dusty darkness. Her hair, freshly combed, shone like spun gold in the morning light, but her brow was furrowed with worry about Patrick Deighton.

She went on, "And you weren't able to find out anything about who might have been involved in the stampede?"

Ki shook his head. "Today I'll try to do some work on that. I'll find out what I can."

"I just hope it's not too late. Whoever did it might be out of town by now."

"But whoever ordered it done is probably still here," Ki added.

"You may be right," said Jessie, distractedly. "Was Patrick hurt very badly?"

"The other man suffered much more than Deighton did."

Jessie sipped her coffee. She said, "I don't like any of this. I'm going to see Weatherby today. He was nice enough last night—that is, he didn't talk down to me in front of his guests." She told Ki what she had learned about the priest, Father Patetta. "You were right. He's the one to watch. The prince seems not very bright—a decent man, but malleable. I looked in my father's diary yesterday, before the party. There's no reference to Prince Klaus von Stumpf, or anyone by the prince's surname. I don't think he's involved with the cartel—at least not knowingly. I'm not so sure about the priest, though."

"I'll talk to the girl again. She may have more to tell me."

"Something tells me we don't have much time, Ki," Jessie said. "Weatherby put me off once—and he never gave me a a good reason. This time I'm not going to be put off, no matter what he says. Not that I very much want to do business with him, especially after what Patrick told me about him. But I think I had better keep a very close eye on him. After all, he may be the one responsible for last night's fiasco at the yards."

"As long as Deighton doesn't blow up and cause more trouble on his own. He is operating on a very short fuse, as they say." Ki sipped his tea. He was not reluctant to give Jessie advice when he thought she would profit by it. "You'd better speak to him, too. He respects you; he'll listen to you."

"I'm glad he's on our side," she said, thinking of that night she had spent with the handsome cattleman, hoping there would be more times like that.

• • •

Weatherby kept Jessie waiting for a quarter of an hour. When his secretary escorted her into the plush office of the bank president, Jessie was simmering. She was wearing her riding outfit this morning—a brown skirt, a white cambric blouse open at the neck, knee-high boots with small-roweled spurs. She carried a leather bag in which she had put her peachwood-handled .38 Colt revolver. She was in no mood to be trifled with.

"Good morning, Miss Starbuck," Weatherby said cheerfully. He was neat, as usual, in his serious banker's suit with his tightly knotted cravat and gleaming gold watch chain. His every movement betrayed a self-satisfied air that made Jessie want to slap his face.

"Good morning, Mr. Weatherby," she replied shortly. "Thank you for dinner last night. I enjoyed it very much."

"You were a lovely addition to the affair," he replied. "The prince was most favorably impressed. He told me so himself. I'm sorry you had to leave in such a hurry. Did you and Mr. Deighton solve the problem at the yards?"

"No, we didn't solve anything. We still don't know who was responsible for the destruction. Luckily, we didn't lose any cattle, nor was anybody hurt. We got there just in time to prevent major damage."

Weatherby folded his long fingers into a steeple beneath his chin. "That is good to hear," he said, with just a hint of disappointment in his voice. "Who knows how much damage the cattle could have caused if they had been allowed to stampede into the business district? Quick thinking on your part seems to have saved the day."

"There is work left to do. The corrals will have to be repaired, the cattle recounted just to be doubly sure none were lost. And—most importantly, in my mind—we must find out who did it."

"I, for one, hope you find out soon," Weatherby volunteered. "It does none of us any good to have such criminals on the loose, with nothing to do but cause mischief."

"I hope mischief is all there is to it, Mr. Weatherby."

"What else could there be?" Weatherby wondered, raking his fingers over his smooth chin.

"Surely," he went on, "you don't think it is anything other than that. What would anyone have to gain by such a senseless act?"

"I have no idea," Jessie said. "Except perhaps to disrupt the deal that Patrick Deighton and I were on the verge of working out for the sale of my Circle Star herd. But I can't imagine who would be against that deal. Can you?" Her bright green eyes bored into Weatherby. She was giving him a lot of rope, wondering if he would wind up hanging himself with it.

But the banker was slippery. With a shrug of his shoulders he said, "I certainly cannot, either. It is unlikely that anyone in his right mind would pull such a transparent stunt. That is all there is to it, it seems to me—a stunt."

"Whatever it was intended to be, it certainly cost me time and money," Jessie said.

"That is to be regretted," Weatherby sympathized. "If there is anything I can do to help you, all you need do is ask, Miss Starbuck. I shall be happy to be of assistance."

"If you had been willing to talk to me when I first came to this office, I'm sure none of this would have happened. I'm here today to complete the financial arrangements I outlined in my proposal to you. Have you considered it?"

"Indeed I have," the banker said. He sat back in his big leather chair, toying with an unlit cigar, regarding the pretty woman in her riding outfit. "It is a very good proposal, Miss Starbuck. I am impressed."

"I am not here to impress you or anybody else, Mr. Weatherby. I am here on business."

"I appreciate your frankness, Miss Starbuck. A rare quality in either men or women. In my years in the banking business—"

"Pardon me, Mr. Weatherby, I don't wish to be rude, but I didn't come here this morning to hear about your years in the banking business. I came to learn whether or not you are interested in financing my purchase of a stockyard operation."

Weatherby raised his eyebrows. Here was an impatient—some would say an impudent—young woman; needless to say, he was not used to dealing with her like. He said, "Well, in a word, I *am* interested, Miss Starbuck." He punctured the tip of the long cigar and put it to his mouth. He struck a match and lit the cigar with several long puffs. He went on, "There are only two factors preventing me from saying yes right now. First, you must sell your herd for a good price, in order to have the capital to invest in this proposed venture. Second, I will have to meet with my board of directors in order to get their approval in this matter. I think they would want to be consulted."

Jessie was just about ready to boil over. "I don't believe you have to consult your board of directors, Mr. Weatherby."

He assumed a shocked look. "Are you doubting me, Miss Starbuck?"

"Yes I am. I can't figure out why you don't want my business. But apparently you don't. Or at least you want to make me beg for your support. And that I will not do."

"You are misreading me, I assure you," he said. "Having done business in the past with your late father, I very much want to do business with the Starbuck family. However, I cannot circumvent bank policy in order to satisfy personal whim or desire. Surely you can understand my position."

"You don't make it easy, Mr. Weatherby," she said. Jessie went on to tell him that she had met Penland at Guarantee Trust and come away with a much firmer offer. "Why can't you give me a definite answer?"

A glint of malice lit Weatherby's eyes, but he controlled his temper. "You are free to solicit and to consider any such offer you may receive," he said. "I shall be able to make you an offer myself within another few days. There is nothing that says you have to wait for my institution to sew up your account."

"It was because of my father's relationship with you that I wrote you in the first place. Now it sounds to me as if you really don't care whether you continue that relationship with my family."

"As I said," Weatherby insisted, "I want to do business with you. But on my own terms."

Jessie said, "Then why won't you just tell me what those terms are? I'm looking for a straightforward business arrangement, profitable for both parties. I really don't care about what you want or don't want. All I need is a yes or a no."

Weatherby shifted in his chair. The smoke from his cigar curled up in front of his face. "Perhaps you are too young to realize, Miss Starbuck, that such decisions are rarely so cut and dried."

"I am old enough to know exactly what I am talking about," Jessie blazed. "And I realize when I am being treated like a child, Mr. Weatherby!"

She rose to her feet in one swift movement. She was about to wheel and walk out of the banker's office when she checked herself. *Be careful,* she reminded herself. *Don't let him rile you.* After all, based on what Patrick Deighton had told her, Weatherby was possibly involved in last night's strike at her herd and his yards. She must not let him get the upper hand; she must keep the lines of communication open. Otherwise she'd be out in the cold, without any way of knowing what Weatherby was up to.

"I assure you, Miss Starbuck—"

"I'm sick and tired of your assurances," Jessie said, controlling her voice. "I require a definite answer from you within twenty-four hours, or else I will take my account to Guarantee Trust and have done with you. That is, I trust, not too much to ask."

"You are a volatile young woman," Weatherby said. "I would caution you against acting without considering the consequences."

Jessie frowned, and leaned across Weatherby's desk. "Is that a threat?" she asked the banker.

"It is not," he said. He consulted his watch. "Forgive me, but I have another appointment."

"Goodbye, Mr. Weatherby," Jessie said as she turned and marched out of his office.

After waiting two hours, Ki was rewarded for his patience. The girl, Heidi, emerged from the hotel lobby onto the street. She turned in his direction and he waited for her. When she saw him, her face lit up. "Hello," she breathed as he approached.

"Hello, Heidi," he said, taking her arm gently. He guided her away from the traffic of the street and onto the sidewalk.

Her blue eyes widened with expectation as she followed him to the mouth of an alley. "You are not going to try to do bad things to me, like that man did?" she asked teasingly.

"Of course not," said Ki. The remembrance of their time together, however, was very vivid in his mind. "Not out here, in this place."

"Ki, I have missed you. I want you to come to me again. When can you—?"

He put a finger to her lips. "Be quiet. Don't talk of such things now. I need to hear of other things."

"What do you want to know?" she asked.

"Tell me about last night. Did anything unusual happen? Did you see Father Patetta at all?"

"I helped the princess prepare for the dinner party at the banker's house. She and the prince and Father Patetta left the hotel together before eight o'clock. They returned at around midnight. There was nothing unusual . . ." She paused, thinking a bit harder, trying to remember.

"Was there something?" Ki encouraged her.

"Well, I would not call it unusual, really," she said. "But there was a man. I saw him before they left for the party. He was talking to Father Patetta. Then he came back, after they returned."

"Did he speak to the priest again?" Ki asked her.

"Yes he did. Just for a minute, I think. In Father Patetta's private room. I don't know what they talked about."

Ki asked her to describe this man.

She did. He seemed unremarkable, no particularly distinguishing features. He was of average height, well dressed. That was all she could remember. Ki tried to picture him, tried to place him among those he had seen since coming to Kansas City. There was no match to be made. "Had you ever seen this man before?" he asked.

Heidi hadn't. "I believe it was the first time."

Ki sensed something about this strange man, but he could not put his finger on it. "Where are you going now?" he asked her.

"I must purchase some soap for my mistress. She says she does not have enough soap for the Grand Tour. She wants to be very clean when she meets the Indians."

Ki could not help chuckling. "Many of the Western tribes prize cleanliness very highly. She will be welcomed by them, I am sure."

The girl looked askance at the handsome samurai. "I think you joke with me. I must find the soap for my mistress."

Ki accompanied Heidi on her shopping trip. He had two reasons for staying with her: first, to insure that she was not attacked as she had been two days ago, and second, because it was such a pleasant place to be.

This morning, Kansas City was bustling with activity. The streets were crowded with men and woman going about their business. Carriages cluttered the wide streets, and the cracking of buggy whips could be heard above the clatter of hooves and wheels on cobblestones. It was unreasonably warm, and bright. Heidi wore a gray shawl over her shoulders and a long blue dress that set off her beautiful eyes. Ki admired her from every angle.

With the soap safely in hand, she and Ki visited some of the other general merchandise stores. She was amazed at the quantity of goods that were available, all under a single roof. In her country, she said, there was nothing like it.

As he accompanied her, Ki tried to stay as inconspicuous as possible. After having been indirectly involved in last night's fight, he knew he might not be a welcome sight to many folks. Also, his escorting this beautiful German girl might raise some eyebrows. So he played it safe, keeping in the background, hovering near, but not too near.

Heidi sensed Ki's unease. "Is something wrong?" she asked him finally, when they were on their way back to the hotel.

Ki told her about last night, about the trouble at the yards, about the fight Deighton had been in at the saloon. "Jessie is meeting again today with Jason Weatherby, the banker. She doesn't like Weatherby and neither do I. But we can't figure how he and the priest are involved, or if he had anything to do with the trouble last night. There's no direct link."

She looked puzzled. "Why would a rich man act like a criminal, or cause trouble for other people? He is rich, he will not starve. What more does he want?"

"I've never been able to answer that question," Ki said.

Taking his arm, Heidi said, "I think you are a good man, Ki—very smart and very kind. Will you come back with me to my room? I—I want to talk to you some more."

The invitation was touching. Ki knew that he had struck a chord in this girl's heart—as she had in his own. "What will your mistress say?" he wondered. "I don't want you to get in trouble with her."

"Do not worry about the princess," said the girl. "She will be taking a nap soon. She really does not get out of bed until very late afternoon. I have never seen a woman sleep so much. But that makes it good for me: I am able to get my chores done without interference from her. She will not even know you are there."

Nonetheless, Ki decided not to enter with Heidi. Instead he found an entrance in the back of the hotel—through the kitchen—by which he was able to gain access to a service stairway. He found Heidi's room without a problem.

She waited for him by the door, allowing him in, then closing the door quickly and fastening the lock. When he was inside, she threw her arms around him. "I love you, Ki," she breathed, her blue eyes sparkling with desire.

The samurai escorted her to the couch and sat down beside her. "I can't promise you that we'll be together after this," he said. "I don't want to lie to you. I think you're a beautiful young woman and I'm happy to be with you now. But—"

This time she put a finger to Ki's lips. "Do not say it. I know what you mean—and I want you anyway, Ki." She kissed him on the lips.

Ki pulled away. "Also, you are my eyes and ears here. You must keep watch on the priest for me. You must find out where he goes, who he sees. And—if you can—find out who the man was who visited him twice last night."

"Do you really think Father Patetta is up to something evil?" she wondered aloud. The idea of a priest, a holy man, involved in any form of illegality was, to her mind, close to blasphemy. Even knowing Patetta as well as she did, she did not want to accept the possibility.

Ki said, "Heidi, at this point I suspect everybody and trust no one—except you. Jessie and I are strangers in this town. We don't know who our enemies are—if indeed there are any. Ever since her father's murder, she and I have been under attack by evil men who wish to destroy her. These men will stop at nothing; they will corrupt a priest or a serving girl—anyone who can do their dirty work."

"I would not wish to have enemies like that," the girl said.

"You're lucky that you don't."

"I am lucky that you are my friend," she said, her eyes blazing into his.

He said, "Do you know where the priest is now?"

"No," the girl said. "I have not seen him since last night—before he went to the party with the prince and the princess."

"You didn't see him when they came back?"

Heidi thought for a moment. "No, I didn't. But that is not unusual. Sometimes I don't even see the prince, just my mistress. The priest is not always with them."

Ki considered this, wondering if it held any significance. What relationship did the priest really have with Prince Klaus? With the princess? From all he could gather, Ki believed that Father Patetta led a mostly independent life. Serving the royal family—having made himself invaluable—seemingly gave him a sort of immunity, the ability to move where he wanted, when he wanted. Did the prince, for instance, know that the priest was meeting with Weatherby? Very likely, Ki thought. According to Jessie, the prince considered Patetta his most trusted advisor. But at night, when the prince was safely in his bed, what did the priest do then, and where did he go?

He turned to the girl. "Will you do something for me, Heidi? Will you keep a close watch on Father Patetta—tell me where he goes, as best you can, and when he goes. I'm interested in whatever you can find out for me."

"Yes, I'll do that for you," she agreed readily, wanting to please him.

"Good," he said. He valued her friendship and respect. He must make certain that nothing happened to her, that she was not hurt by any of this. But she was even more valuable to him if she could help him in this way.

Again she asked him, "How can you think the priest is involved in wrongdoing? I do not like him, but I have never seen a priest or a nun do something wrong."

"You haven't seen much of the world, Heidi," Ki said gently. "There are all kinds of people, good and bad. I'm not saying that the priest is a bad man, but he may be involved in something that will hurt Jessie. If he is, I must stop him. If he is not, that's even better. I must think of Jessie first, the priest second."

The girl nodded. "I understand."

"I want you to understand, to know exactly what we may be up against. It is dangerous sometimes, what Jessie and I do. We don't invite trouble, but often it seems to follow us. And it has followed us here to Kansas City."

"I know," Heidi murmured. "It makes me afraid for you. I would not want anything to happen to you, Ki. I could not bear it." She turned to him and pressed herself closely against him, her hands on his chest.

Ki wrapped his arms around the girl, feeling her warm breasts, her arms, her hands. She lifted her face to his, looking at him openly, longingly. Her eyes were wide, imploring him for love. He said, "Is your door locked securely?"

"Yes," she said in a breathy whisper.

Ki picked her up in his arms. She was light and he carried her easily to the bed in the adjoining room, where he lay her gently. He sat down beside her, feeling the need within himself growing almost uncontrollably. This girl did something to him—he was not sure what. The air between them was charged electrically. He saw that she was breathing more heavily, evidencing her own deep need for him.

"Come to me, Ki," she demanded huskily, her arms outstretched.

He did, bending to kiss her again. Their lips burned

together; he pressed hard, wanting to exorcise some demon from within, wanting to give her as much as she could take.

"Are you certain we're safe here?" he asked, pulling himself from her for a moment.

"Yes, Ki," she said. "My mistress will not want me for a few hours. We have at least that much time together. Please do not go."

"I won't leave you," he said, stroking her flushed face. Then he began to unbutton her dress. She did not protest, but lay still, allowing him to complete the task.

Soon, Ki had succeeded in undressing her completely, and she lay totally naked before his eyes. She was not as shy during this encounter as she had been the first time. Having tasted Ki's love once before, she knew he would be respectful of her body, and at the same time totally uninhibited in his lovemaking. Such a man was different from any she had ever known.

Ki marveled at her body. She was young and smooth, her skin so pale as to compare to the smoothest, whitest marble he had ever seen. As she smiled at him, he saw her face glow with expectation. She moved her body sensuously atop the bed, inviting him to discover its pleasures, its every curve and hollow. Her breasts stood proudly, pink-tipped, rising and falling with her breathing.

His eyes traced the curve of ribs and waist to her flaring hips, which were planted on the bed but seemed ready to move, to lift to receive him. The smooth skin glowed almost pink at the point below her belly where there was a soft rise and fall, and then the golden triangle of tangled hair, so fine it seemed like spun gold. Her legs then tapered down to the foot of the bed, every inch sculpted to perfection.

"What are you looking at?" she teased him.

"Your beauty," he replied simply.

"Why are you looking?"

Ki responded by stripping his own clothes off and joining her on the soft bed, lying full length beside her, one arm over her breasts. He kissed her cheek, her chin, nuzzling at her neck and planting many kisses there. Then he traveled slowly down to her shoulder, her chest, lingering at her budding breasts, teasing them with his skilled tongue.

Heidi sucked in air and moaned in brief spurts, drinking in the many sensations this man exposed her to as he seemed to cover every inch of her body in kisses. "Ki . . . Ki . . . Ki . . ." she repeated, over and over again.

He did not answer her, except to continue his explorations. His tongue traced a hot trail from below her breasts to the soft rise of her belly, lingering at the navel, tickling her there. She laughed, then gasped as Ki moved down to the nest of downy fur at the point where her shapely legs met. She reached down and lightly tugged at his hair.

"What are you doing?" she asked, her accent thickening with passion and alarm.

The samurai answered with a flick of his long tongue. He moved his body down and set himself between her legs, lifting them to allow him better access to her sweet, secret chamber there. He held her firmly as he kissed her soft, slick lips and probed with his tongue, darting in and out like a snake. The girl squirmed and cried out, never having experienced this strange, forbidden form of lovemaking.

That did not stop Ki. Inhaling the pungent frangrance of her love juices, he used the flat of his busy tongue to stimulate the inflamed button that quivered at the entrance to her chamber. Heidi had to stifle a scream of ecstasy as she felt him probe and press with his tongue, causing her to quiver inside, loosening those muscles, making her juices flow even more freely.

"Mein Gött, Ki!" she exclaimed as he inserted his tongue as deeply as he could.

Then he began to flutter the tongue quickly and lightly over the surface of her nether lips, teasing the already throbbing nob above, bringing the girl closer and closer to climax. His neck muscles strained, and he held her legs apart with his strong hands as he worked to give her the utmost pleasure. Within another minute he felt her reaching the brink. Finally she began to buck wildly, moving her hips up and down and around, pressing her sex into Ki's face. She turned her head so that she could scream into a pillow as she came, and Ki felt her love muscles contracting spasmodically.

Moving himself up on the bed, the samurai held the girl tightly. She wrapped her arms around his smooth, naked back. When she showed her face, there were tears in her eyes, and her cheeks were flushed a bright pink.

"Where did you learn to do such a thing, Ki?" she asked in amazement. "I never knew a man could do that to a woman."

"It is not uncommon where I come from. Perhaps it is not allowed by priests and churches in your country, but I cannot understand why."

"Oh, Ki, you make me feel so wonderful—so alive. I want you to love me again. I want you inside me this time. I want to feel you." As she spoke, she reached down and took his stiff sword in her small hand and pumped it lightly. Already he was rigid.

He moved to comply with her request, lifting himself above her. He kissed her again, long and hard, full on the mouth. She kept a tight grip on his distended blood-red rod, as if to let go would mean she would lose it forever; then she opened her legs to him and helped to guide him home. Ki moved with her as she placed the head of his shaft at her moist, love-slicked sheath.

With a mighty thrust, Ki entered her, pushing all the way to the hilt. The girl's mouth opened in a silent O as she took him in. It was tight, but the loveplay had lubricated her adequately, and Ki began pumping rhythmically.

Heidi lifted her legs, wrapping them around the small of the warrior's back so as to hold him there. She opened her eyes to look at him, the dark hair falling into her face, his black eyes blazing, the golden skin shadowed. She pushed her hands up his strong arms, feeling the muscles tensed there, his hands braced on the bed at either side of her shoulders. Meanwhile, he continued to plunge in and out in long, even strokes that drove her wild.

"Do it to me, Ki . . . please . . ." she whispered urgently.

He could not reply, only keep doing what he was doing, with as much restraint as he could muster. She felt so warm, so willing, so tight, so sensual. Her body had become a temple at which he was worshipping the god of love, lost in the darkness that threatened to become the blinding light of release. She moved her body beneath his, lifting her pelvis to meet his long strokes.

Ki gritted his teeth and felt sweat breaking out on his forehead. Heidi, too, was sheened in a patina of perspiration as she tensed, then relaxed, then tensed again with the rhythm of their lovemaking.

Heidi's fingers dug into Ki's shoulder blades, and she gritted her teeth. He saw her hold her eyes closed tightly. He continued to move, quickening his strokes. A lump in his throat told him that he, too, was closer to climax, and he pumped harder. She clung to him, lifting herself from the bed, her legs clamped firmly around him. She tossed her head, squealing, wanting to speak but unable to form the words.

Soon, Ki was lost in a fog of pure sensation, and he could only feel their bodies and smell the heat of their passion. There was nothing else in the entire world—and the only danger was that they would not reach fulfillment. But both of them, like two wild animals in the woods, could not now control the inevitability of their coupling. They held on to each other with desperate need; neither of them would let go.

Then, in a flash of cold blue light that suddenly spurted hotter than the heart of a flame, they came together. Ki choked off a primal howl. She rocked her hips to keep him inside her, and to take each drop he had to give. Her internal muscles contracted, milking him.

With ragged breaths, Ki finally stopped, dropping his lips to hers, fusing them in a long kiss. Her tongue fought his for attention, and he tasted her hot breath. They lay together, Ki's shaft still encased in her, for a long time; neither one of them wanted this moment to end. Heidi stroked his back. Ki regained a sense of reality and disengaged himself from the girl.

"Don't leave me," she whispered. "Don't ever leave me."

Ki found his clothes and began to dress.

★

Chapter 8

Before he left, Ki asked Heidi to tell him where the priest's room was. She told him it was just down the hallway. He kissed her, promised to see her again soon, and cautiously left her room. There was no one else in the hall. As quietly as a cat, he made his way to the priest's room.

His instinct had told him to check on the priest while he had a chance to do so personally, and Ki trusted his instinct. Many times in battle he had saved his own or somebody else's life by following his hunches, as Jessie called them.

He stopped outside the door. Again checking the length of the hallway, he saw nothing. Ki put his ear to the priest's door. He heard talking. He listened more carefully—two voices at least. Tensed, his ear pressed lightly to the door, he put all his energies into listening. The words began to filter through more clearly. Yes, two men were speaking. The one with the Italian accent had to be the priest, while the other one . . . Ki did not immediately recognize the second voice.

"This is probably the best chance we shall ever have, Signor," the priest was saying.

The other man replied, "*Your* best chance, perhaps, but I am not interested in your petty feuding. I am interested only in money. And there is a good chance to make some money here. It is time for me to conclude my business with her, and until I do that—"

"Ah, you say our 'feud' is petty, but your money is of the greatest importance. You Americans are all alike. You put money first, and blood and honor are secondary considerations for you. Well, for me, Signor Weatherby, honor comes first, money second."

It was Jason Weatherby, Ki now realized. Pressing his ear more closely to the door, he found it very difficult to make out every word the two men were saying, but he kept at it.

"That's bullshit, Patetta, and you know it. You care as much about making a buck as I do. You mask it, though, in that priest's gown and talk of honor and blood. I know you well enough to know that you would sacrifice your own mother if it would profit you."

"To speak of my mother thus," the priest said icily, "is blasphemy from your lips, Signor. You will not speak of my mother like this. Upon me you may heap your insults. For myself I do not care. But, Signor—"

"All right," Weatherby interrupted impatiently. "Enough of your moralizing. Perhaps you are too much of a priest. Even though your soul is as black as that robe you wear."

There was a pause. Ki could imagine the priest smiling at Weatherby's characterization. "We were talking about the girl, Signor Weatherby, not the state of my immortal soul."

"Well, I can agree to let you have her, but only after I'm finished with her. You've held me up long enough on this."

"That will be too late. The prince is due to embark the day after tomorrow upon his Grand Tour. I wish to finish with Miss Starbuck before that date. If I report to my superiors that I bypassed this opportunity, they will skin me alive upon my return to Europe. You agreed to delay her stay here, and you have done so. I can see that you are compensated for the time you have spent with her—plus any additional monies you can fairly claim as lost to you. She must be eliminated. That is all I care about. I am willing to pay any price for that."

Ki's blood ran as cold as ice. He could not believe what he was hearing. What had the priest against Jessie? Patetta wanted her dead, and wasn't particular about how it was done. Ki wanted to know the why of it. Who were the priest's "superiors"? And what had they to do with Jessie Starbuck? The possible answers frightened the samurai.

"Well, my boys did a good job last night. The trouble at the holding pens set the girl and her friend Deighton back at least a day." Weatherby laughed. "I hear it was quite a mess down there."

The priest was silent for a moment. Ki could imagine him pacing the floor inside. Then he said, "You rely too much on tricks and diversions. You are so used to deceiving people that you cannot face an honest fight." Patetta let this sink in before he went on, "You could have been rid of Deighton and his father long ago—if you had challenged them face to face and bested them."

"That would not improve my standing in the community," the banker replied. "The Deighton family has friends still—friends who could make problems for me. I cannot afford that, Father."

"You cannot afford to have this young man making trouble for you now."

A pause, and then: "No, you're right." Weatherby was considering the priest's words. "I have let it drag on for too long. But how do I get rid of Deighton?"

Patetta said, "You can work with me. Together we can put both the girl and Deighton out of the way—for good. That will solve problems for both of us."

"I still don't understand what you have against Jessie Starbuck," Weatherby said.

"It is nothing she has done to me personally, but the group of men with whom I deal in Europe—businessmen, bankers like yourself, government men—have suffered at her hands. You see, her father was killed some time ago, and she believes that it is the cartel who is responsible. Whenever she discovers a cartel member or representative, she wastes no time in challenging him. So far, she has won every challenge she has thrown down. But this time it shall be different. I promise you that."

"What exactly do you intend to do with her?"

"What would you do with young Deighton, if you had the chance?"

"I'd kill him," said Weatherby without hesitation.

"Yes, exactly," replied the priest.

Ki could barely contain himself as he listened at the door. He checked the hallway yet again, to be sure he wasn't being watched. Then he pressed his ear back to the door. These two ruthless men were planning to kill Jessie and Patrick Deighton, talking about it as if it were just another business transaction. It made Ki sick to think that they could expect to get away with it. And when Jessie found out... He smiled dryly to himself, knowing what her reaction would be.

The banker was saying, "Are you certain we can do it without being caught?"

"There must be a way. As I said, you are an expert at disguising your intentions and covering up your dark activities. Do you know someone who can do the job for us—

someone who will not talk, under any circumstances?"

"I know some reliable men," Weatherby assured the priest.

"Good. When can we meet with them?" Patetta asked.

"As soon as you like. How about tonight?"

"Yes. The sooner the better."

"I'll notify you as soon as I have gathered them. And—just to warn you—these men may want a substantial deposit, as a sign of our good faith."

"Money is no object, Mr. Weatherby," said the priest.

Ki, his ear pressed hard to the door, trying to concentrate on the conversation inside, did not see the man approaching from the stairway. His heart was racing as he listened to the conspirators in the room, and he forgot to check the hallway again.

The man came up behind him, moving stealthily. He unholstered his revolver and held it butt-forward. Within three steps he was upon Ki. In a single smooth movement he lifted the revolver, then brought it down hard on the back of Ki's head, knocking the samurai unconscious with the blow.

Ki fell forward, his head crashing against the door. Inside, there was a sound of alarm as the two men came running to the door.

"What's going on?" Weatherby shouted.

"Open up," the man said. "Got something here for you to see."

The door opened and the banker and the priest peered outside. There they saw Ki's body sprawling on the floor. They opened the door wider to allow the man to drag Ki inside. His breathing was ragged, and a ribbon of blood trickled from his scalp, where the gun butt had broken skin.

"It's the Starbuck girl's friend," Weatherby exclaimed. "Where did you find him, Egan?" he asked the man.

"Right outside. He was listening by the door," Egan said.

Weatherby turned to Father Patetta. "He must have heard what we were saying." The banker's face was pale. "He would have reported to the girl if Egan had not stopped him."

The priest said, "It was the will of God that he not inform her." He looked from Ki to Egan to Weatherby. "This bodes well for us, I think. We can use this to our advantage. The girl is very attached to the Oriental, from what I understand. Now that we have him, we have her, too."

"I don't follow," said Weatherby, wiping his forehead with a handkerchief.

"Don't be dense, man. And do not be frightened. If we tell the girl—through a third party, of course—that we have her friend, she will be forced to come to terms with us. We have her in the palm of our hand, Signor." The priest was smiling now, his dark eyes dancing; this was the moment he had been waiting for. Ever since he had learned that Jessie Starbuck would be in Kansas City, he had worked to put her against the wall. Now she was there.

This reassured Weatherby somewhat. "Yes, that makes good sense. But who will this third party be? How will we contact her?"

Exasperated, Father Patetta said, "Did you not tell me that you know certain men who will take care of this matter for the right price?"

"Yes, of course," the banker replied.

"Then we shall call upon these men. They can take the Japanese to a safe location outside of town, keep him there securely and quietly. Then they will find the girl, demand a ransom, force her to come looking for him. And, no doubt, Mr. Deighton will go with her. Side by side, they will be—what do you Americans call it?—yes, 'sitting ducks' for us. Do you agree with my plan, sir?"

"Yes, by God," the banker said, regaining his confidence. "Egan, did you hear what the padre said? I want you to bring this man out to the farm. Get in touch with Blanchard and Manley. Tell them I need at least six men to guard this fellow around the clock—and then I want you to report to me for further instructions. Understand?"

"Yes sir," Egan replied.

"Get going, then," Weatherby ordered.

After her fruitless meeting with the banker, Jessie spent the afternoon with Patrick Deighton. He showed her around his meat-packing and shipping operations, then took her out to the country, where he and his father maintained a small ranch. He was feeling a bit sore, and more than a bit rueful, over his battle of the previous night. He told Jessie all about it, saying, "I guess I was looking for a fight. Something inside me wanted to get out."

Having heard the story from Ki as well, she understood. "Don't think about it, Patrick," she reassured him. "Just too bad you couldn't do some damage to whoever is really responsible for the mess at the railroad yards."

"I thought about that," he said. "In fact I probably should be working on that, instead of squiring you around out here in the country."

Although it was cool, the sun was shining and the air smelled of brown grass and golden leaves. She was enjoying it, enjoying the time away from the town and the time with Deighton. He controlled the reins of the buggy with his left hand, while his right arm was around her shoulder. She sat close to him. She wanted to do more for him, to help him in his fight against Weatherby—if only she knew how.

"Ki is doing some detective work for us today," she said. "He'll have some information when we get back. You deserve a few hours away from town. I'm glad you took me along, too." She edged closer to him, putting her arm across his chest. Taking a deep lungful of fresh air, she felt cleaner than she had in days—since she and Ki had first come to Kansas City.

"Hope he doesn't get in trouble," Deighton said, as the buggy followed a rutted trail.

"So do I," she said absently.

Soon, Deighton was driving her in the direction of a big, rambling farmhouse. A dirt road wound up a small hill toward the house, and the young man followed it as if he had taken it many times in the past.

"Where are we going?" Jessie asked.

"You'll see," he said mysteriously, a twinkle in his eye.

Within several minutes the buggy had taken them to the front steps of the house. Deighton jumped out and came around to assist Jessie. She stepped down and looked around at the big house and the land surrounding it. The house itself was two stories tall, solidly built of brick and stone, with a wide veranda stretching across the front. From the hill where it stood she could see in all directions for a great distance. To the north and east was pastureland, dotted with cattle; to the west was a wooded area, with leaves on the trees flaming various colors; and to the south she could see the Missouri River as it rolled mightily across the plain.

She turned to Deighton. "It's beautiful," she murmured.

"It belongs to my father and me," Patrick Deighton said. "Come on inside."

Jessie followed him into the house, through the front door and directly into a large foyer. It was dark and somewhat musty-smelling inside. There was little sign of life here. But she did smell woodsmoke. She turned to her companion, who stood looking around the place with a sad look on his handsome face.

"This is your place?" she asked.

"My father built this house practically with his own hands," he said. "He lives here now. I want you to meet him."

"I'd very much like to, Patrick," she said. *It must be difficult for him,* she told herself. *This house must hold a lot of memories—good and bad—for him.* She could see it in his face.

Deighton took her hand and led her up the main stairway, which dominated the right side of the foyer. The stairs wound up to the second story. He took her to one room and paused for a moment outside. "My father is a sick man," he said to her. "He still has his mind, but he is weak. I try to see him often—even though it hurts me sometimes. Are you sure you want to—"

"Of course, Patrick. I'd love to meet him." She reached up to pull his face down to hers, and kissed him on the mouth. Then she went into the room with him.

A fire was crackling in the fireplace on the west wall, and a man sat in a tall chair, wrapped in a blanket, near the fire. He did not look up when the two entered. Patrick cleared his throat and moved toward the old man. At that, the elder Deighton looked up.

Jessie could see in that face many years of suffering. Mr. Deighton looked older than his years, his face a map of wrinkles and creases, a sallow yellow color, and his hair growing in wispy white tufts. As he reached out a hand for his son, she could see that he possessed long, slender fingers that were now wrinkled and spotted with age and illness. His hand moved slowly but steadily toward the young man, who took it in his own.

"Dad, I brought someone to see you," young Deighton said.

The old man turned, squinting to see Jessie. She came forward and took his hand and shook it. "It is my pleasure, Mr. Deighton. Patrick speaks of you all the time."

"He talks about me too much, you mean. He should learn to live his own life and forget about the old man." He squeezed her hand with surprising strength. His watery brown eyes were focused surely upon her—admiring her fresh, youthful beauty.

"Singing the same old tune, Dad?" Deighton said wistfully.

"Hell, yes, son. I've told you—what happened to me is ancient history. Now is *your* time to live. Forget about the past and think about the future—before it's too late." He turned to Jessie and winked. "Now, young lady, tell me if that is the truth or just the ranting of a senile old man. You look like a smart girl."

"Of course it's true, Mr. Deighton. But Patrick respects and admires you. I'm sure he'll be successful in whatever he does. He owes that to your example. Isn't that right, Patrick?"

The big man nodded. "Listen to her, Dad. She makes sense."

The old man laughed, a rasping sound from deep inside his lungs. He probably did not laugh very often these days. Then he seemed to consider something; he looked Jessie over from head to toe. "Did my son say your name is Starbuck?" he asked.

"Yes," she said.

"Any relation to old Alex Starbuck?"

"He was my father."

"I'm awful sorry, young lady, about what happened to him. He was a good man—one of the old breed. They don't make 'em like Alex anymore." His eyes took on a distant, dreamy cast. "He didn't take orders from any man—he gave orders and others jumped. I didn't know him very well, mind you, but I heard about him—plenty. I imagine that's why he was backshot—because some folks got riled at his success." He shook his head. "I have seen it happen to other men."

"I've seen it happen to you," Patrick Deighton put in.

"Maybe it did, maybe it didn't. I think now I brought it on myself. I wasn't tough enough. I trusted too much. I let that dadblamed Weatherby get his claws into my skin, and I couldn't get them out. I can still feel it..." His voice trailed off as he gazed into the fire.

"Dad, you should be in town to see Weatherby's latest catch—a genuine prince from Bavaria. Kansas City's all agog at the royal personage. You've never seen anything like it."

The old man managed a dry, crooked smile. "You can be sure there's some dirty deal in it—if Jason Weatherby is involved." He pulled the blanket closer around his waist. "It's awful damned cold in here, don't you think?"

Jessie said, "Patrick, why don't you fetch some more wood?"

"Hear that?" Deighton said to his father. "She's ordering me around like a slave."

"Well, do what she says, boy," the old man groused, with a wink at Jessie.

When Patrick was gone, Jessie pulled up a chair and sat down beside Mr. Deighton. "Has he told you what's been going on in the last few days?" she asked him.

"No, he doesn't tell me anything anymore," Deighton said bitterly. "He thinks it will make me angry and cause my blood to boil and make my heart give out. I couldn't care less about that. I do want to know what is happening. So tell me, young lady."

Jessie outlined the events of the past few days, since she had arrived in Kansas City. The old man listened with fascination, interrupting her a couple of times to ask pointed questions. When she was finished, she asked him what he thought.

"You know what my answer will be. I think it's that goddamned Jason Weatherby behind your troubles last night. And I know why he's holding out on your proposal to buy into a stockyard—because he thinks he can cheat you out of some of your money. He'll charge you an enormous finder's fee or some other imaginary service fee. I'm glad to see that you have decided not to trust him."

"He decided that for me," she said. "Just by the way he

handles his business. At first I didn't think he was taking my proposal seriously."

"Anything to do with money, he takes seriously," the old man cautioned her. "What I'm curious about is how he got involved with this prince fellow—and the priest. Sounds like there's some big deal brewing there. I've never seen a priest in cahoots with a banker, though. What do you make of that?"

Jessie told him what she thought. "My friend Ki is trailing the priest now, trying to find out what he can. I met him last night and couldn't get a straight answer out of him. My intuition is that he's up to no good."

"Trust your instincts, girl," Deighton advised her. "You can't go very wrong that way."

"That's what Ki says. And I've found that he's right most of the time."

"Sounds like a remarkable fellow, this Ki you keep talking about."

"He is," she said. "Remarkably resourceful. He's like a brother to me."

"So what are you going to do about Weatherby—and this priest, if he is involved?"

"I'm not sure, Mr. Deighton. Unless I can catch him red-handed, prove somehow that he was involved with the stampede last night, I can't very well take him to court. Even then it would probably take weeks, maybe even months for a trial. I don't know . . ."

"Take an old man's advice, Miss Starbuck. If you can punish Weatherby and his henchmen outside a court of law, do it. I don't believe in lynching, as a general rule—but for Weatherby, a rope around his neck is all he'll understand."

"You're right," she said. She liked this man; he had lived a long time, seen many things. She could trust his advice. At times like this, Jessie felt her father's absence most keenly. In her life there was no one to whom she could turn to talk things over, to seek help; except for Ki, who was not that much older than she, she had no man to advise and protect her. She envied Patrick Deighton his father.

Patrick returned with an armful of firewood, dropping it near the fireplace and rebuilding the fire there. "What did you two talk about?" he asked.

"None of your goddamned business," the old man said.

"We didn't talk about you, if that's what you're worried about," Jessie said.

"The only thing I'm worried about now is that I'm going to starve to death," Patrick Deighton said. "Dad, is there any food in the house?"

"Look in the kitchen, son," said Mr. Deighton.

"Come on, Jessie, help me fix something. If we have to listen to the old man's rantings, I at least want to do it on a full stomach."

"Just bring her back, that's all I ask," the father teased. "I don't get to see such a lovely girl every day. I'll give you credit for that, my boy."

Jessie blushed. "Thanks, Mr. Deighton."

The young man said, "Come on, Jessie. I swear I'm starved!"

A thick, coarse rope bit into Ki's wrists. As he regained consciousness, he felt the pain there and at the back of his head, where he had been cracked with the revolver butt. He stirred. He was enveloped in darkness; it was difficult to breathe. Lying on his side, he could see only a sliver of light perhaps three feet long and an inch wide. Then he realized where he was—in a closet, probably in the priest's room.

His head felt as if it had been split open like a pumpkin. His mouth was dry, and his back was bent. He was hogtied like a calf being readied for branding, and every muscle in his body was strained. God, what he wouldn't give for a drink of water! But he knew there was nothing he could do about that—not in his present condition. He cursed himself for his carelessness. He had no one to blame but himself.

He tried to remember just when it had happened. He had been listening to Weatherby and the priest plotting against Jessie. Twice he had checked the hall for intruders, and it had been clear. But the one time he had neglected to check, someone had come upon him and taken him out easily.

What would Jessie think if she found out?

Shifting his weight as best he could, Ki managed to maneuver himself closer to the foot of the door. Straining to put his face there, he tried to look out, but he saw nothing. He could hear movement, though. It sounded like more than one person in the room—perhaps as many as four or five. Their voices were low, and they mingled almost inaudibly. Ki was unable to make out any distinct words.

Meanwhile, he turned his attention to his bonds. Whoever had tied his wrists had done a good job, and the remaining length of the rope was wound around his waist, keeping his wrists pinned to his lower spine so that he had absolutely no freedom of movement. He could not swing his hands around to the front to try to gnaw at the rope with his teeth. There was absolutely nothing for him to do but lie there and wait for his captors to come get him.

He did not have long to wait. The closet door swung open and bright light spilled into the enclosed space, causing Ki to squint to keep the light out of his eyes. Then he felt two hands grab him by the shoulders; he was hoisted up and out of the closet.

The man deposited Ki on the floor at the feet of Father Patetta and two other men. Ki looked up into the priest's hard face. Patetta gazed impassively upon the prisoner, his eyebrows twitching. He said to the three men, "I wish to spend some time alone with this man. Wait outside until I call you again."

The others exited, leaving only Ki and the priest.

"I believe your name is Ki. I am Father Albino Patetta. I have met your employer, Miss Starbuck, but it is an equal honor to meet you, sir. Your reputation is a fearsome one, in certain circles."

"What circles?" Ki managed.

"Ah, it is not for you to ask questions, Signor Ki. That is my role. You might say I am the Grand Inquisitor here." He laughed shortly, showing his long white teeth. "My superiors in Europe are very interested in your activities in the United States—both you and Miss Starbuck. Therefore, it behooves me to ask you to describe those activities."

"I'll tell you nothing," Ki spat. With his head turned awkwardly upward to see the priest's stern face, the words came out strangled. He would not allow Patetta to steal his dignity or to make him reveal *anything* about Jessie.

"I believe you shall, Signor Ki. My faith is strong." The priest stepped closer to the hogtied samurai. His robe concealed the movement of his feet. He continued, "You will not disappoint me. I ask you again—tell me about Jessica Starbuck's activities against the cartel. How much does she know? Does she know names?"

The throbbing of his injured head caused Ki's vision to blur. The bonds cut off the circulation of blood in his arms and hands, and those limbs felt numb. The priest's words, though, came through clearly enough.

"I'll tell you nothing," Ki repeated adamantly.

"That is too bad for you. Do you believe in God, sir? Surely you will tell me that."

"I believe in the gods of my people. Those gods are strong, as are my people. We have never been conquered."

"A martial spirit. I admire it in you, sir," the priest went on. "Well, I am telling you, you will be praying to your gods before the day is out. For, sir, I shall extract the information I want from you—by whatever means necessary. Do you understand my meaning?"

Ki understood perfectly, but he did not say a word.

Deftly the priest reached down and took a fistful of Ki's long, glossy black hair. He yanked it savagely. "You are not a stupid man." He jerked Ki's head so that they were face to face, the priest hovering above, menacingly. "Does the girl know I work for the cartel?"

Ki said nothing.

Patetta slapped Ki's face, a quick, stinging blow with the front of his hand. Then he brought the hand back, raking his knuckles across the other side of Ki's face. Ki winced in pain. His entire spine felt as if it were wrenching from its sockets.

"Talk," the priest commanded. But Ki kept his mouth shut. Again Patetta slapped him, and again, until he drew blood from Ki's nose. Then he dropped Ki's head; it crashed to the floor. With swift accuracy the priest planted his boot toe in Ki's lower back.

Ki's brain exploded with pain. Helpless, he was at the evil priest's mercy—of which there was a short supply. Slowly his eyes fogged over. He could hear Father Patetta quietly asking him once more to spill his guts.

Again the boot swung into his back. Slowly a black curtain descended on Ki, as another blow sent him spinning into unconsciousness.

★

Chapter 9

Jessie was silent for most of the trip back with Deighton from the visit with his father. It was late afternoon now, and the fading sun trailed off to the west as the air grew more frigid. She wrapped a blanket about herself and sat close to Deighton, who also did not volunteer any conversation.

Then she said, "In a way, this reminds me of the Circle Star—this wide-open land, the air, your house."

"I like it all right. Except that it's not as wide-open as all that. Even out here, Weatherby has gone up against my dad. Over to the east"—and he pointed to a broad area of the shadowed land—"Jason Weatherby has a big estate, much of it formerly Deighton land. During my father's business troubles, he had to sell off several hundred acres to Weatherby."

For a long time Jessie watched the land that passed before her—again silent. How did Patrick Deighton really feel about his father? she wondered. She knew he was fiercely proud of the old man's accomplishments, equally bitter about Weatherby's attempt to break him. The way he talked about his father told her that he loved the old man very much. She could understand. After all, she still felt the same way about her father, even though he was long dead. To her, Alex Starbuck was as much a presence in her life as if he were alive. In a way she envied Patrick that—his father was alive and able to give back some of the love the son gave him.

The beautiful countryside unfolded in front of her eyes. Here, close to the river, there were steep hills dotted with trees; and the road, such as it was, wound snakelike up and down these hills, through flaming arbors and across the fading grassland. A cold autumnal breeze blew into her face, bringing out the red in her cheeks, bracing her.

Breaking the silence, she said, "How often do you visit him, Patrick?"

"Often as I can." Deighton kept his eyes trained on the road, the reins held steadily in his hand. "He's gotten worse lately. The doctor says it's his heart. He still hangs on, though. It's almost as if he didn't want to die—ever. Or at least until he can see that his enemies get what's coming to them."

"He's a smart fellow. I'm surprised he wasn't able to keep Weatherby down."

"My dad's only problem is that he's honest through and through. Smart, yes, but he plays fair. That's not Weatherby's way—the banker will do anything to get what he wants. Dad just won't."

Jessie said, "Why didn't my father know this about Weatherby? Why did he do business with him?"

"Maybe he didn't know, Jessie. Or he never had a chance to tell you."

"I suppose. What with him getting killed like that, there were a lot of things we never got to talk about. I just wonder if somehow the cartel has got to Weatherby, or is using him. He may not even know he's their tool."

"Oh, he'd know, all right," said Patrick Deighton. "He might keep his mouth shut, but he'd do what they said and take the money."

She knew he was right about that. It only served to deepen her suspicions, to make her more anxious to find out what Ki had discovered today.

Deighton drove her back to the hotel and helped her down. They stood looking at each other for a brief moment.

Then she said, "Would you like to come upstairs?"

The young cattleman squeezed her hand. "Yes," he said. "I'll park this buggy and be right up."

In a few minutes he knocked on her door and Jessie let him in. They embraced tightly. He searched for her lips and found them, crushing his own against hers. She was small and almost fragile in his large, strong arms, and he had to be careful not to hurt her as he held her.

She pushed him away, laughing. "This cool weather sure makes you hot," she said.

"You do that to me, Jessie. Only you."

"I wonder where Ki is," she said distractedly. "He should be back by now. Unless he's onto something important."

"I hope he doesn't come back for a while," breathed Deighton.

"Oh, Patrick—" she kissed him loud and hard. "You're like a little boy with his hand in the candy jar."

"I can't get enough, if that's what you mean."

"That's exactly what I mean." He took her in his arms again, and reached behind him and locked the door. Then he swept her up into his arms, and carried her to the bed. "Jessie, I want you so bad."

"Patrick," she murmured as he bent over her. They kissed, lips and tongues melding sweetly, and she felt his hot breath on her face. "Yes, Patrick. Come to me." She opened her arms and her lover came into them, and the two entwined on the bed in a hot embrace.

Within a few minutes, Patrick had helped her strip her clothes off, and he struggled to free himself from his own. His shirt and pants and boots joined hers on the floor beside the bed. She lifted the bedclothes and he joined her beneath them.

Jessie pressed her body against his, feeling the masculine hardness of his legs and torso. He was a big man, and she liked that. She ran her fingers through the matted hair on his broad chest, luxuriating in the feeling. "Don't you have other girls, Patrick?" she asked him, curious to know more about his life.

"Nobody to speak of," Deighton replied. "I've been with a few other women. Mostly they're pretty silly. They're after my money or my name—they don't know any better."

She laughed. "I'd go after you, too, if I lived here. Like all the others. Do you think you're going to get married someday?"

"Is that a proposal?"

Jessie slapped playfully at him. "Absolutely not. I'm not going to get married for a long, long time. But I asked you—are you going to settle down and raise a family and all that?"

Deighton considered the question. His dark eyes bored into hers and there was a trace of a smile on his lips. "If the right girl ever comes along. If she has shining red hair and a soft, shapely body—then I'll consider it. But not till then."

"Quit joking. I'm serious, Patrick. I want to see you happy. Wasn't your father happy with your mother?"

"Very happy. It nearly killed him when she died."

"But he had you. I'm sure he was grateful for that."

"For all the good I've done him." Deighton pulled his arm away from Jessie. He spoke in a low, bitter tone. "Jessie, I feel that I've let the old man down. Weatherby is still running around causing trouble, cheating people, making himself rich. And what have I done? After he just about drove my father to his grave—"

"Stop it, Patrick. Don't talk like that." She cupped his chin in her small hand. "You've been a good son. I can tell that he loves you very much, that he's glad to have you for a son. Don't blame yourself for something that's not your fault. Weatherby will get his—and soon. I feel it in my bones."

He allowed her to pull him closer, bringing his lips to her face. He kissed her there—her eyes, nose, cheeks, lips, chin, nuzzling at her ear until she squealed. He wanted to devour her, every inch of her. Never before had he met a woman with such energy, such intelligence, such beauty, such desirability. He felt foolish, but at the same time he felt more like a man than he ever had before. God, he wanted her...

"Oh, Patrick," she cooed. "I want you to be happy. I don't want anything bad to happen to you ever again."

"Make love to me, Jessie. That's all I want. I ache for you."

She reached down, groping at his crotch, until she found the evidence that he was, indeed, aching for her. His rod stood up stiffly at attention as she wrapped her fingers around it, feeling its hardness and warmth. She pumped it lightly, moving her hand up and down its length.

"Oh God, Jessie!" he choked.

"Relax, Patrick," she whispered. She wanted him to enjoy and savor their lovemaking; she wanted him to feel totally and completely a man.

Raking her free hand across his chest, she found his nipples and bent to take one in her lips and suck on it gently. It quickly grew erect and she grazed her teeth over it, causing the young man to cry out. It was a sensation he probably had never felt before she had done it to him. The time before, when they had made love, she had discovered these little but important things about him. Now she wanted to put what she had learned to good use. She attacked the other nipple, teasing it and causing him to gasp for breath. All the while she kept a firm grasp on his distended organ.

Then, kissing his chest, she slid down to kiss his lower torso and glide her tongue down its length. Deighton, surprised, did not know what she was up to, but he could hardly speak. He watched the lovely mane of red-gold hair descend, and he stroked her shoulders.

Soon Jessie's face was at the place where his swollen sword jutted from a mat of tangled black hair. Slowly, building momentum, she swirled her tongue around the base of the pole, all the while squeezing rhythmically with her skilled hand. Then she flicked her tongue against the sensitive skin there, licking at it like a child with a candy cane.

Patrick Deighton sucked in air. "God, girl—what the hell are you doing?" he asked.

Jessie did not answer, but just attended to her ministrations. She ran her tongue the entire length of his organ, from base to tip, and back down again. With the tip of her wet tongue she traced the ridged veins and tickled the red, distended skin there, teasing him unmercifully. Then, without warning, she lifted her head and put his manhood between her lips.

"Jesus!" Deighton hissed.

Slowly, bit by bit, she took in as much of him as she could, lowering her face toward the base of his shaft. Lifting her head, she then plunged down again, taking the slick organ in more deeply this time. Up and down she bobbed, holding the tumescent base firmly in one hand, letting her lips do the work.

Deighton grabbed a handful of her golden hair, trying to control her movement, but he could not. Jessie knew exactly what she was doing, and wanted nothing more than to please this young man and show her affection for him. She knew no better way than this.

"Holy Christ, Jessie!" he moaned. "Oh—please—God! What are you—" He could not finish the thought; a wave of pleasure crashed over his mind, nearly blinding him.

Jessie worked his shaft with her lips, sucking strongly and pumping him. She felt the shaft tense and knew he was approaching orgasm. Then she lifted her head and pinched the base, closing off the way. She moved up on the bed, and Deighton took her in his arms.

He kissed her, almost violently. "Jesus, girl, I've never felt anything like that before. Now I know why none of the girls around here are worth it."

Jessie said, "Hush, Patrick, I want you to come inside me." She rolled over on her back, pushing the bedclothes aside. The late sun fingered weakly through the window, casting a dim glow on the two lovers. Patrick climbed over on top of her.

She reached down and took his long, steel-hard manhood as he positioned himself between her outspread legs. She guided it home, then, inserting it gently, feeling it slide in. Already she was lubricated, ready for him.

Deighton rammed it in all the way, feeling her delicious tightness. He wanted to cry out—to curse, to praise heaven, to scream in both pain and delight. But all he could do was pump his blood-engorged sword into her willing sheath. He opened his eyes and saw her there beneath him, her beautiful pink-tipped breasts heaving, her mouth open, her hair spilling over the pillow like a raging fire. She lifted her legs into the air to give him freer access to her, and he lengthened his strokes, slowing, then quickening his pace.

Her green eyes blazed as she saw him looking down at her. She reached up and grasped his strong shoulders, squeezing them. The big man bulled her with all his strength and she wasn't sure she could take it. But she gritted her teeth and opened herself to him. His big shaft nearly split her in half; she wanted to make him stop, but knew she couldn't.

"Oh, Patrick!" she gasped. "Please . . . yes . . . give it all to me . . . yes!"

He gave her all he had. Together they bucked like a pair of mountain cats in heat. Jessie pushed her pelvis up to meet his ramming weapon, and Deighton pushed home again and again into her steaming chamber. Soon they reached the point of no return.

She felt herself go liquid, and her head spun wildly. She tried to gulp air, but her lungs were not capable of taking in enough.

Deighton, meanwhile, reached the brink. With the beautiful girl writhing beneath him, he could hold back no longer. He emptied himself into her. Every drop he had came spitting out through the rigid shaft with which he rode her.

He collapsed into her arms. Both of them were breathing heavily, trying to regain a sense of reality. But it was not easy.

"Patrick . . . you know how to make a girl feel real good inside," Jessie finally managed.

"Jesus, Jessie, you're the one who tied me up in knots. I was only doing what I had to do." He smiled and kissed her. "What would my dad say if he could see us like this?"

Ki was a mass of bruises. Not a square inch of his body was without pain. The priest had worked him over thoroughly, trying to extract information from him. But the loyal samurai had not said a word. Now Father Albino Patetta was frustrated. He had never before encountered a man who would not talk after some time with the boot.

"Son of the devil," he cursed, as Ki rolled over, wincing.

Ki's mind reeled as he tried to hold onto consciousness. He had blacked out three or four times during the priest's interrogation, and he did not want to go under again. If only he could stay awake and aware, he would be at least even with the game. The only weapon he had was his mind. There was no way he would talk if he knew what was happening around him. He thought of Jessie, wondered if she knew he was missing. She wouldn't hesitate to put herself on the line to get him back; he knew that, and it made him angry. If he could keep his thoughts focused on her, perhaps he could hold out.

"I have dealt with pagans before," the priest muttered. "You are not the first, nor the last, Signor Ki. I will break you—or my friends will. One way or another, you will tell me what I wish to know." He went to the door. "Blanchard, Manley, come in here."

Through a painful haze, Ki saw two pairs of boots move into the room and heard two voices.

"He is being stubborn," Patetta told them. "He thinks, no doubt, that he is outwitting me, but he will learn differently. I want you two men to take him to a safe place outside of town. Signor Weatherby mentioned a farm house you sometimes use."

One of the men spoke. "Yeah, where some of the boys hole up after a job, Padre. We can keep him safe and sound out there."

"Well, that is where I want him, then. We do not have much time. I am scheduled to meet with the prince in an hour. Can you smuggle this man out without raising suspicion?"

"Done it before," the same man said. The second man seemed to prefer not to speak.

Ki wanted to get a good look at their faces, but he could not lift his head high enough to catch a glimpse. His head hummed with pain, and he could barely see, anyway. Then he felt hands lifting him by his arms. Even there he felt tender, bruised by the priest's expert treatment. He wondered where the cleric had learned such worldly skills.

The samurai was deposited on a couch that gave softly

beneath his weight. He was now able to lift his head. Through the mist he saw the priest's black soutane, saw him pacing the floor and gesturing with his hands.

"I want one of your men to deliver a message for me. He must be someone you can trust—someone not well known in this town. This is a very delicate job."

This time the second man spoke. "We have the man you need." His voice was more even, more cultivated than the first man's. And Ki thought for a brief moment that he had heard the voice somewhere before.

"If all goes well, there will be a nice reward for you two gentlemen. Signor Weatherby will see to that." The priest sat at a writing desk and began to write scratchily with a pen.

Ki calmed the wild thumping of his heart, trying to regain his senses. He closed his eyes for a minute, then opened them again. His sight was slightly improved. He tried to focus on Father Patetta, and nearly succeeded. The cleric's face was clearer to him. He looked up at the two men who stood nearby. It was more difficult to see their features, because both of them wore hats. The effort just to see exhausted the battered samurai. Again he closed his eyes.

Patetta finished writing his message and inserted it in an envelope and sealed it. He rose and handed it to one of the men. "This must be delivered to the Hotel President at six o'clock sharp. But first you will transport this man to the farm house. Is that understood?"

"Yeah, Padre. Loud and clear," said the first man.

"Good," said the priest. He walked over to Ki. "I am not finished with you yet, my good man. You and I shall talk again. I look forward to it."

Ki looked at him, expressionless. His vision was returning. He did not give the priest any indication that he had regained full consciousness. He turned his attention to the other men as the priest turned his back.

The bigger man was unshaven, with curly gray hair beneath his hat. He wore an open-necked flannel shirt and black denim pants. There was nothing remarkable about him that Ki could see. But the second man—shorter, more slender, neatly dressed in a gray suit—caught Ki's attention. He wore a stylish gray hat, pulled low over his face. He was clean-shaven, his features smooth. And he looked familiar. Ki knew he had encountered the man before—but where? When?

"It will take us about forty minutes to make it to the farm," the second man said. "The message will be delivered to the hotel precisely at six, as you wish." He reached into his vest pocket and removed a gold watch attached by a long chain.

Then it struck Ki—a conductor's watch! This man was the conductor on the train Jessie and Ki had taken to Kansas City! He was the one who had come to their compartment after the fight with the two intruders. Somehow he had been connected with that attack!

Jessie and Deighton dressed slowly, after they had lingered in bed for nearly an hour. They had made love a second time, driven by an almost uncontrollable passion that they could not deny. Now, though, it was nearly sunset, and they had to get back to business.

Her brow was furrowed as she buttoned her blouse. "I should have heard from Ki by now. What time is it, Patrick?"

"Nearly six o'clock. You mustn't worry about Ki, Jessie. He can take care of himself."

"I know that, but—" The words stuck in her throat. "If anything were to happen to him, I'd never forgive myself for it."

Patrick Deighton took her in his arms once again. "Nothing will happen to him," he assured her.

"Oh, you're right," she conceded, planting a kiss on his chin. She helped him button his shirt. "I just wish he'd come back. I'd feel a lot better."

They were dressed and ready to go when there was a knock on the door. Jessie looked to Deighton. "Who the—" she wondered aloud.

He moved her to one side, unholstering a big .44 revolver from his gunbelt. Jessie had already pulled out her converted .38 Colt. He called, "Who is it?"

"Message for Miss Starbuck," came the reply.

Deighton opened the door to the messenger. He was a nondescript fellow who handed over the envelope and left. Deighton watched him go, and reached back to hand Jessie the letter. He closed the door and locked it carefully.

"What's it say?" he asked as he holstered his revolver.

Jessie went pale. "They've got Ki," she said woodenly.

"Who's got Ki?"

"I don't know. Read this." She handed him the letter.

He read it aloud: "'Dear Miss Starbuck, Your companion, Mr. Ki, is presently in the custody of a third party. He is still alive and well. However, he shall not remain in this condition unless you cooperate fully with our instructions. For now, you are to do nothing. You are to await further communication from us. Any attempt on your part to notify the law will result in Mr. Ki's death. Surely his life is worth quite a bit to you. Therefore, we expect you to act in his interest by obeying us. We shall communicate with you again tomorrow. Be prepared to meet with us then.'

"Who the hell is this?" Deighton spat. He tossed the letter aside. "The goddamn bastards. Weatherby is behind this!"

"Don't go jumping to conclusions, Patrick," Jessie cautioned. "He may be and he may not be. My first concern is for Ki."

"They say he's still alive—if we can believe that."

"We've got to believe it."

"Sure, Jessie. What do you suggest we do?"

"If possible, we must locate Ki. When I saw him last, he was on his way to see the girl who works for the prince and princess. He talked to her before—she was giving him information on Patetta, the priest." She took up her hat. "We'll talk to her first."

"I'm right behind you," Deighton said as they exited the room.

At the royal family's hotel, Jessie stopped at the desk and asked for Princess Therese. The clerk informed her that Her Highness was taking an afternoon nap at this time and was not to be disturbed. Jessie controlled her temper, but just barely.

"This is very important," she explained. "I wouldn't dream of disturbing her if it weren't. I must talk to her."

"Well . . ." the clerk hesitated.

Deighton said, "What room, mister? That's all we want."

He directed them to the royal suite, reluctantly, apparently expecting the prince's wrath to descend on him for this breach of trust.

Jessie and Deighton bounded up the stairs, arrived at the royal suite, and pounded on the door. A dignified old man with immaculate white whiskers and a waxed mustache opened the door and inquired in a thick accent as to their business.

"We must speak to Princess Therese immediately," Jessie said. "It is very important."

"The princess, she naps. It is before dinner. Cannot be disturbed," the man said.

"Listen, mister," Deighton put in. "We're very sorry to disturb her, but it can't be helped. We must see her."

"It's a matter of life and death," said Jessie.

"Well, I—" the servant began.

Then, behind the old man, Jessie saw Prince Klaus approaching, tightening the sash on a silk smoking jacket.

"My dear Miss Starbuck, what brings you to us this evening?" He was smiling brightly. He acknowledged Patrick Deighton with a nod and ordered the aging servant aside. "Come in, both of you," he invited.

Jessie wasted no time. "I must see your wife, Prince Klaus. I want to talk to one of her maids. The girl named Heidi."

"Heidi, yes," said the prince. "She is attached to my wife. You wish to speak to her? My wife, you see, is indisposed."

"Yes, we know," Jessie said, exasperated. Never had she encountered such solicitous behavior toward one human being by so many others. For God's sake, it was only a nap! "If we do not have to awaken Her Highness, that is fine. As long as I can speak to the girl—immediately."

Prince Klaus turned to the servant. "Eric, please find Fräulein Heidi, and bring her here at once."

"Jawöhl," the old butler said. He bowed crisply and stalked off to find the girl.

"Please, make yourselves comfortable," the prince offered. "Would you care for tea—or something else to drink?"

"No thanks," Jessie said. She could not drink or eat anything until she knew more about what had happened to Ki. She could barely stand still, waiting for the girl, so impatient was she to begin trailing her samurai companion. If they had done anything to Ki, if they had hurt him at all, they would pay dearly, she vowed.

Presently the old man returned, with the girl in tow.

"Heidi?" Jessie said. Heidi looked at her, wide-eyed. She had never seen an American woman quite like Jessie Starbuck. All the ones she had observed were laced up tight, not like this young woman in riding clothes.

"Yes, I am Heidi," she managed.

"I am Jessie Starbuck, Ki's friend. You know Ki."

"Yes..." The girl blushed slightly, but kept her composure. "We have met. Herr Ki—" Then it struck her. Jessie was distraught. Why was she asking about Ki? "What has happened? Is Ki in trouble?" Her eyes betrayed her concern.

"We do not know what happened, Heidi," Jessie told the girl. "That is why I have come to talk to you. Ki said he was going to see you today. Did he?"

"Yes," Heidi said. "He came by to talk to me."

"When?" Jessie demanded.

"This morning. We—we talked for quite a long time."

"When did he leave you?"

"I don't know what time..." the girl said, her eyes darting from Jessie to Deighton. She tried to think. She felt the prince's eyes upon her, and tried to put that out of her mind. "It must have been after noon. My mistress called me to her room an hour later."

Jessie looked at Deighton. "That was over five hours ago. Who knows what could have happened since then."

She said to the prince, "I am going to ask Heidi something you may not like, but I want you to bear with me." He screwed up his face, wondering what on earth she could mean. Jessie then turned to the girl. "Did Ki ask you about Father Patetta?"

"Yes," Heidi said. "He asked me many things about Father Patetta."

"Were you able to tell him what he wanted to know?"

"I think so. What Father Patetta has been doing, who he has seen, that sort of thing. I told him what I knew."

"Where is the priest now?" Jessie asked.

"I do not know," the girl said.

Jessie asked Prince Klaus the same question, and he replied with the same answer.

She cursed under her breath, then turned to Deighton and said, "That doesn't give us much to go on." To the girl she said, "Is there anything else you can remember? Did Ki tell you where he was going after he left you?"

"Well, he asked me which room was Father Patetta's, and I told him. From my room he went there. I do not know how long he stayed, but I saw him listening outside the priest's door."

"Miss Starbuck, I say, this is highly unusual!" the prince fumed. "Do you mean to say that your man was spying on Father Patetta, my trusted friend? This is intolerable! I would not have expected such behavior from you or your associate."

"I am sorry, Prince Klaus," Jessie said. "But you will understand my actions when we are able to straighten this out, believe me. I beg your indulgence for the time being."

That soothed the prince's ruffled feathers a bit. "Very well," he said skeptically.

"Patrick," Jessie said, "go with Heidi. I want her to take you to the priest's room. See if he is there. If not, find out where he went. Do you understand, Heidi?"

"Yes, ma'am."

"Good, be off, both of you." She then said to Prince Klaus, "Your Highness, I think you and I had better sit down and talk about this matter."

He ordered tea and sat with Jessie on the long sofa, his hands in his lap. She explained, as best she could, her suspicions concerning the priest. Urging him to keep the entire matter confidential, she even told him about the cartel, how it operated, and what were its aims. He listened without expression on his face. For a moment Jessie wondered if, indeed, he was a member of the cartel. But she decided that he could not be; he was too naïve, too well-meaning. That, she surmised, was why the priest was able to manipulate him so easily. He looked as surprised as she had been when she told him about the letter informing her of Ki's kidnapping.

"We must find your friend," the prince stated flatly.

"I'll take any help I can get."

"But tell me more about Father Patetta. Why do you suspect he is involved with this cartel of businessmen? He is a priest, a man of God."

"You said yourself, Prince Klaus, that he makes many of your financial decisions for you. I believe he uses his priesthood to cover many other activities. It may be difficult for you to see that now. But I have a hunch he is somehow involved with Ki's disappearance."

Deighton returned. "Patetta went out just a half hour ago. I checked at the desk, and the clerk said he went to meet with Jason Weatherby."

"Damn!" Jessie's fist hit her knee. She shot a glance at the prince. "You're probably not used to such language—sorry."

"No," Klaus said with a brief smile, "it is refreshing to hear a woman speak her mind. Sometimes I wish my Therese did."

Jessie drained the rest of her tea. "Let's go, Patrick. We have a long night ahead." She rose and extended her hand to Prince Klaus. "Thank you for your hospitality—and for your understanding. We won't be back to bother you again."

"It is no bother, my dear Miss Starbuck. I hope you find your friend."

"We will," said Jessie.

★

Chapter 10

Outside, disappointed that the prince had had nothing concrete to tell them about the priest, Deighton turned to Jessie. "I have an idea," he said.

"What is it?" she asked, eager to know anything that might help her samurai companion.

They stood on the sidewalk, and a cold breeze whipped across the street, which was dark now. She stood close to the big man, ignoring the evening chill. All she could think about was Ki.

"Just a thought," Deighton said, "but if Weatherby is in any way involved in this, and he wants Ki out of the way until you come to terms with the kidnappers, then he'd want Ki out of the city—right?" His voice was edged with excitement.

"I suppose so."

"Then where to take him? What better place than Weatherby's ranch out in the country—next to my dad's property?"

Her eyes lit up. "Maybe... maybe."

"It's worth looking into," Deighton insisted.

"You're right," Jessie said, deciding right there that it would be worth a try. "But we'd better be well prepared if we go in. If they're holding Ki, they'll be guarding him tightly."

Deighton said, "I'll meet you at your room in about an hour. I'll get hold of some guns and ammunition."

"We don't want to take the buggy, do we?" she asked, only half joking.

"I'll get us each a horse, too," he said.

"Right," Jessie concurred. On her tiptoes, she deposited a kiss on his cheek, then ran the few blocks to her hotel.

Once in her room, she quickly changed her clothes, putting on a heavy shirt, a vest, denim pants, and riding boots. Then she sat down on the bed with her weapons, to clean them.

First she broke open her cherished .38 Colt, a present from her father. He had had a fine, sturdy, single-action .44-caliber revolver converted to take a .38 load, the gun's large frame effectively absorbing the recoil of the lighter load, making it more suitable for a woman's hand. After breaking the weapon down, cleaning it thoroughly, and giving it a light filming of oil, she loaded five rounds into its chambers, leaving the empty one under the hammer in case of accidents—a trick she had learned from her old friend, Marshal Long.

Then she removed from its leather case a gleaming .44-40 Winchester and gave it the same careful treatment she had given the Colt.

Satisfied that her weapons were ready, Jessie strapped on her gunbelt and holstered the converted .38 Colt. Into a pocket of her waist-length leather jacket she stuffed a pair of supple gloves, and into the other pocket she put boxes of cartridges for both guns.

Yet, even as she prepared herself as well as she could for a possibly violent confrontation, she felt the icy chill of impending danger stab at her. She wanted to cry. They had Ki, damn it! And she wasn't even sure who *they* were. It would be Weatherby, or the priest, or anybody who knew she would pay any ransom, or even give up her own life, for his survival. He meant more to her than any person living. She would not let him be harmed if she could help it.

Her eyes misted as she thought of all the times she and Ki had been together. She remembered the danger they had shared, the days beneath the open sky with the sun beating down on them, the hours of work at the ranch, their travels to places all over the West. Together they were an unbeatable team, she knew. To her enemies, Jessie and Ki presented a united front that could not easily be penetrated. But apart—she did not know how effective she could be alone against the cartel or anybody else. She had never considered how to fight them without Ki.

Impatiently she awaited Patrick Deighton. She was relieved, at least, that he would be at her side in the search for Ki. She hoped his hunch was right—that Ki was being held at Weatherby's country place. It made sense, after all. That is, if Weatherby was involved. Still, that didn't answer the most important question. Where had Ki been when he was taken, and who had actually taken him?

Thinking back over what the servant girl, Heidi, had told her, Jessie figured that Ki was in or near the hotel when he was kidnapped. He had last been seen by the girl on his way to the priest's room. Somehow, she thought, he must have stumbled onto something he wasn't supposed to see, or exposed himself too openly as he was tracking Father Patetta.

It occurred to her that it was possible Ki was being used as a pawn. Perhaps she herself was the object of the kidnappers' efforts. Ki was the next best thing, of course, Jessie realized. Wherever he was, she was close behind. Perhaps they weren't going to ask for any ransom; perhaps they were going to ask for her. She shuddered at the thought.

At times like this, Jessie cursed her Starbuck heritage—for it was because of that name, that wealth, that reputation, that Ki was in trouble this night. Always, men wanted something from her—money or pleasure or a piece of that name. Thinking that as a woman she was "defenseless," they often resorted to stupid tricks that only endangered them. Too late, they found out that she could take care of herself very well, especially with Ki siding her. This kidnapping, she suspected, was just such a move by a hidden enemy.

Soon enough, she vowed, she would unmask that enemy and make him pay for his mistake.

Deighton came for her, and she went out with him to the street, where he had two horses waiting. He mounted the tall bay and she swung onto a slightly smaller sorrel mare. The saddle was comfortable, equipped with a scabbard for her rifle, into which she slid the weapon.

Already it was dark, and clouds obscured the moon and stars. Jessie was glad she had dressed warmly and pulled her hat securely down onto her head. Her horse did not seem to mind the late autumnal chill, though it blew gusts of vapor from its nostrils. With these thoughts about the cold, Jessie tried to occupy her mind as she and Deighton rode out, but with little success.

"Patrick," she said, "do you really think Ki is there?"

"Hell, Jessie, there's no way of knowing unless we go in there and find out. If he is, we'll get him out, don't worry about that."

"I am worried," she admitted. "We don't know how many men will be guarding him, if Weatherby or the priest are there, if he's hurt or unconscious. We don't know anything."

Deighton reined in his big bay. They were outside of town now, picking their way carefully along the road that led northeast toward the Deighton property they had visited earlier. Jessie caught up with him.

"What's bothering you?" he asked her.

"I'm just worried sick," she said. "If they've hurt Ki or—"

"Don't even think about it, Jessie. We'll find him—tonight or tomorrow or the next day. And when we do, we'll punish whoever it is who had kidnapped him. I promise you that."

"Okay, Patrick," she relented. "You're right. I know it. But I still can't help thinking about all the things that can happen to Ki. He's my very best friend, always has been. Without him, I'm not a whole person. Can you understand what I'm trying to say?"

"I think so," said Deighton. "I respect Ki, Jessie. I know how close you two are. You know, I'd like to be your friend, too. These past few days . . . I've never felt as close to any woman as I have to you. You're something special . . . different from anyone I've ever known." He looked directly into her eyes. "I love you, Jessie Starbuck."

"Don't say it, Patrick. Don't say it right now. Wait till we've done our job. Then maybe we can talk about it." She saw the look of disappointment on his handsome face. "I don't mean to hurt you," she went on. "But now isn't the time. Please, Patrick."

"Sure, Jessie." He reined his horse around. "Let's get moving. We have a long way to ride, and it's awfully cold out here."

She spurred her mount forward, following Deighton's lead. Through the heavy curtain of darkness, they rode in silence for a long while. Only the sound of the horses' hooves could be heard as they clopped in the trail dust.

Trees grew densely on either side of the trail, muffling whatever noise they made. Jessie breathed deeply of the cold, bracing air and it made her feel better. But she couldn't get Ki's predicament out of her mind.

As much confidence as she had in Patrick Deighton, she knew that he was only one man—and she herself only one woman—against an unknown enemy. She hoped that Patrick's hunch would prove accurate, that they would indeed find Ki at Weatherby's estate.

Ki, meanwhile, wondered where Jessie was and if she knew that he was being held prisoner. In fact, he wondered where he was. A few hours earlier, the priest had ordered him blindfolded and packed off—no doubt through a back exit of the hotel—to a wagon that had bumped over a long, rutted road for what seemed like forever. When they had arrived at their destination, the men had roughly unbundled him and tossed him into a dark room—larger than the closet where he had been, but no more comfortable.

He tried to calculate just how far out of Kansas City he was, how long he had been a prisoner, and how many men now guarded him. Having slipped in and out of consciousness several times, he didn't find it easy. He also wondered if the priest—or Weatherby—had yet contacted Jessie with whatever absurd demands they would present for Ki's safe return. He hoped she wouldn't overreact, that she wouldn't lose sight of their motives, which were simple—to get her into their clutches, and then to destroy her.

He knew she would be angry and would want to come after his kidnappers immediately, but he counted on her good sense to prevent her from doing anything too foolishly dangerous.

Ki's body ached tremendously—from the blows he had suffered from the priest during the "inquisition," from the awkward position his bonds had forced him to take, and from being bounced around in the back of a wagon on the trip to this latest location. His head swam in pain, and he could see little in the darkness, with his vision clouded as it was. It took all the courage he possessed, and recollection of his samurai training in his native land, to overcome the pain and confusion and anger he now felt. He thought back on Hirata, and the many teachings the experienced *ronin* had shared with him. The noble Hirata had himself many times been captured by enemies—and each time he had survived. This remembrance gave Ki some hope with which to face the darkness.

Outside the room, Ki could not hear much activity. So, instead of worrying about what he could not control, he decided to find out what he could about the room where he was being held. Fighting the throbbing pain in his head, he tried to maneuver himself toward a wall or some upright object. It took several minutes, but he finally succeeded in dragging his body to a wall. Catching his breath, he lifted his torso up and propped it against the wall. As he moved, he had to be careful not to choke himself with the rope that was looped tightly around his neck. Whoever had tied him had done a damn good job of it.

Then, as he fought to keep his balance, he heard voices outside the door. Footsteps passed, the voices faded, and he heard no more. So he was guarded by at least two men—perhaps as many as four or five. It did not matter; all that mattered was that he was their prisoner.

There was no way Ki could stand, but by hugging the wall he could move around the room, if he did so carefully. By now his eyes were more accustomed to the lack of light in the room, and he peered around. He could make out some dark shapes, but that was about all. He moved to his right, slowly, until he bumped into something that felt like a table. He moved away to his left, until he reached what seemed to be the door. Scooting slowly in the same direction, he passed the door and found himself in a corner. Turning the corner, he groped as best he could along that wall. He collided with a big, immobile object: it was a bed, he realized. So he was in a bedroom.

This, then, was a home, some distance from the center of town—in what direction, he couldn't know—it was no doubt a big country house. Whose? Well, if the priest and Weatherby were involved in his being here, it was likely Weatherby's house. That made sense—if nothing else about this mess made any sense at all.

Ki was angry. Not only had they hogtied him like a branding calf, but the priest had done his best to torture information out of him, and now he had been trundled off to this house far outside of town, where Jessie was unlikely to find him. He was even angrier when he thought of what she must be going through, not knowing where he was. He silently cursed the priest who represented the cartel—another fact that Jessie did not yet know. Well, somehow he'd get out of this mess, get to Jessie and warn her, and then together they would go after the priest, and then Weatherby. But how to free himself from these bonds and gain his freedom?

Propped up against the bed, his breathing becoming easier, Ki contemplated possible solutions to his dilemma.

Then it occurred to him. It might work! His captors had taken the *tanto* he had been carrying. But that was not the only weapon on his person; he had packed two *shuriken* throwing stars in his vest poscket. And if they were still there . . .

Slowly, carefully, he lowered himself on his side. The *shuriken* stars would be in a left breast pocket, tucked securely away. Having achieved a full-length position on his side, he brought his knees up, slackening the noose around his neck and giving him a bit of leverage. Using his knees, he tried to tilt himself onto his left shoulder. He could barely lift himself, and he fell facedown onto the floor with a thud.

Ki held his breath. Had anyone heard him? He waited

several minutes. It seemed no one had. So he started all over again.

This time he was better able to balance himself, and to lift his lower body a few inches more. His left shoulder ached with the weight he placed on it against the bare floor. He jerked his chest, trying to open the pocket and dislodge the throwing stars. He cursed himself for the care with which he had placed them there, to prevent them from being jarred loose accidentally.

He lowered himself to the floor once again. He had a new idea. This time he shifted himself around so that he could catch his feet on the bed frame. Then, slowly, painfully, he edged himself closer to the bed, pulling with his heel hooked onto the frame, getting his ass as close as possible to the bed. It took what seemed like an hour to get where he wanted. Lifting his legs as high as he could without strangling himself, he was able to put his feet over the top, onto the mattress, and slide his shoulder in and under the rest of his body—until he was hanging almost vertically from the bed.

Now, using his bent legs as a grip, he held himself in position. He was able to lift himself slightly and jar his shoulder against the floor. In this way he hoped to loosen the *shuriken* blades and make them fall free. Once, twice, he jerked himself up and let himself fall against the bruised shoulder. He stopped, breathed deeply, and for a third time he lifted himself, jarring the shoulder. As he came down hard, he heard the clink of metal on wood—the blades had fallen out onto the floor!

It took him several more minutes to lower himself quietly from the awkward position he had struggled to take. Finally he was able to get his legs to the floor, assuming once again a full-length horizontal position. The throwing stars lay at his shoulder, so he had to slink like a caterpillar over the razor-sharp blades until he could reach them with his hands.

Again, the process was laborious, taking long slow minutes to accomplish.

In the darkness he groped with his numbed fingers for the blades. He knew he had to be extra careful not to cut his fingers to ribbons. He pricked a thumb against one of the *shuriken* stars, muffling a cry of pain and surprise.

Then, with a feeling of triumph welling up inside him, Ki had one of the precious stars in his hand!

Holding it by a single point, he twisted his body into a position that enabled him to attack the rope that ran tautly from his neck to his wrists. With excruciating care he applied the sharp blade to the line, slicing it strand by strand. Sweat broke out on his forehead as he worked, feeling the razor edge cut into the rope. Finally the rope snapped—he had cut it! The pressure on his neck was relieved. He longed to rub the rope chafings there, but he could not; he had more work to do. Now he gripped the *shuriken* in his fingers and clawed at the rope that bound his wrists, driving the point in and, with a sawing motion, beginning to cut the strands there.

Deighton raised his hand, halting Jessie. Her horse came up next to his. He pointed ahead, through the darkness. There, about a hundred fifty yards in front of them, were several lights. Squinting, she could see that they were windows. A house—Weatherby's house. Her heart raced. If Ki was in there, if he was hurt in any way, Weatherby would pay.

"There might be guards outside," Deighton was saying. "If so, we've got to be extra quiet and careful from here on in. I suggest we picket the horses here and go in on foot."

"Good idea," Jessie concurred. "We don't want to take a chance on alerting them."

Off the roadway, they tethered the two horses to a tree. She joined Deighton, the Winchester hanging from her right hand. He carried a big Springfield .44-40 repeating rifle, slung in the crook of his left arm, ready to do its work when necessary. Jessie watched Deighton move, and her confidence in him grew. He knew what he was doing, possessed a lot of common sense. Even if he had never attacked an enemy position at night like this, he seemed instinctively equipped to do it right. She, on the other hand, had been here only too often—and she didn't enjoy it one bit. Still, she knew what to do, knew it wouldn't be easy, no matter how intense the resistance at the house.

The wind whistled through the dry leaves of the trees, covering the sound of their footsteps and allowing them to approach without sparking an alarm. Keeping their eyes and ears peeled for possible watchmen outside, they moved to within forty yards of the house without encountering a soul.

Jessie whispered to Deighton, "Looks like they're all inside—whoever they are." She still couldn't be sure that Ki was in there, or that he was alive, nor could she know how many men there were.

Deighton nodded. "That's lucky for us. If we can get to the house without being spotted, that'll be half the battle. We'll have to split up, though."

"I'll take the right," she said. "We should make a complete circuit of the house, then regroup out back."

"Okay," said Deighton. "Let me go first. You cover me. I'll wait at the corner there to cover you until you reach the house. Ready?"

"Yes," she said. She watched him dart out across the open ground that was spottily lit by the various window lamps that were glowing in the house. He made it safely, and then signaled for her to make her move.

Bent low, her rifle balanced easily in her hand, Jessie scurried into the open, her eyes absorbing the details of the house. She counted ten windows at the front, two stories, a wide front door and awnings around the front porch. It was a solid fortress, built of stone, meant to last. When she had achieved the safety of her corner, she waved to Deighton.

She then turned and, hugging the wall of the house, began to move toward the back. She took her time, stopping every few steps to listen for anyone who might have been on watch; she heard no one. At one point she came to a lighted window. Pausing to check that she was safe, Jessie approached the window and, standing on tiptoes, was able to peek inside. It looked like a sitting room, and there was one man who stood in front of a marble fireplace, stoking a blazing fire. His rifle lay against the mantel. She shifted her position so that she was able to see another part of the room, and there she spotted another man, smoking a cigarette, watching the fire distractedly. Neither man looked to be too worried that they might be attacked tonight.

This reassured her. At least, if she and Deighton kept the element of surprise on their side, they had one advantage to play against the men inside. These two couldn't be the only ones to worry about, though. She moved on, coming on two more windows but unable to see anything inside. The house was big, and it took her several minutes to traverse the length of this side, taking her time and moving as silently as possible.

Turning the corner, she encountered almost total blackness. The trees grew very close to the house, casting their black shadows over everything there. Only a single light shone from an upstairs window, which gave her something to go on, a point from which she could gauge her own location. She moved along the back of the house to the halfway mark, as best she could judge, and waited for Deighton.

He was along within a minute, looming beside her.

"Well, did you see anything?" he asked her.

"No," Jessie said. "Not outside, at any rate. There are at least two men inside, in the sitting room. They look pretty relaxed."

"I saw another man in the kitchen, making coffee," said Deighton.

"That's three, at least. The odds aren't too bad, so far," she murmured.

"Still, we're outnumbered—and we don't know yet for sure if Ki's in there at all. Did you recognize either of the men you saw?" he asked her.

Jessie hesitated; it hadn't even occurred to her at the time. There *was* something vaguely familiar about one of the men she had seen in the living room, the one stoking the fire. "Wait here for a minute," she told him.

Stealthily she went back to the lighted window, hugging the house all the while, staying in the impenetrable shadows. She wanted another look. She couldn't be sure . . . but somehow she thought she had seen that man before.

Again she lifted herself up to look into the window, taking care not to be seen by those inside. The man by the fire had his back to her. He was about average in height, dressed in a neat gray suit. His rifle still lay canted against the mantel, and he seemed to be talking to the second man, who lay casually on the couch. They did not seem to be overly concerned about what they were doing.

The question still gnawed at Jessie: *Was Ki their prisoner?*

Then the man she was watching turned, showing her his face. Where had she seen him? She gazed at that face . . . and then it struck her. Of course, on the train! He was the conductor who had come to their compartment after the confrontation with the two unknown bushwhackers. But this puzzled her even more. What was the train conductor doing here in Weatherby's house? Or, alternatively, was he actually a train conductor—had he, in fact, been Weatherby's man all the time?

She shrank away from the window and made her way back to the rear of the house, where Deighton awaited her. An idea was dawning on her, and she didn't like it: the man had been a plant on the train, had allowed the bushwackers to board and to attack Jessie and Ki. It had been the perfect set-up. She hadn't suspected a thing all along; this answered the question of how the attack had been executed. But why? Had Weatherby himself, or someone close to him, authorized the attack?

Jessie was ready to spit, she was so angry. All along, she and Ki had been extremely vulnerable. And, stupidly, she had allowed Ki to walk right into some sort of trap. She could kick herself for her carelessness.

She told Deighton what she had seen, that she recognized the man. "He was on our train; he was the conductor," she said. "At least that's what we thought he was at the time."

Deighton said, "Sounds like a set-up, all right. But why would Weatherby try to get you two out of the way before you even got to Kansas City? I can't see him throwing away all that potential money like that."

"Could have been somebody other than Weatherby."

"Who?" Deighton wondered.

"Our friend, Father Albino Patetta?" Jessie said.

Deighton knit his brow. In the chill darkness, his breath came in smoky gusts. "I'll be damned," he muttered. "Maybe it *was* that blackhearted padre."

"We can't know for sure—yet," she reminded him. "Unless we can make the man talk."

"That's not going to be easy. I'm not even sure how the hell we're going to get into this house."

Ki kept working. He had severed one rope, allowing him to move his hands with more authority. The knot was well tied, and Ki had to sweat out two more pieces of rope before the bond fell free of his right wrist. With a sigh of relief, Ki brought his hands around to the front. In the darkness, he could not see the bruises and dried blood around the wrists, but he didn't care. Within another minute he had both hands free of the rope.

Quickly he put the blade to the ropes around his ankles. He clenched his teeth as he felt the sharp tine of the *shuriken* star cut through the thick rope. He applied steady pressure, slicing through strand after strand until—with a snap—the rope came apart. He unwrapped his ankles and rubbed them.

Never had he felt so relieved to be free—though he wasn't completely free yet. He still faced his captors, whoever they were. The only one he knew was the man whom Patetta had called Manley—the phony train conductor. He would like to have had a word with that fellow. He wanted to know what the connection had been between Manley and the two attackers on the train.

But the task at hand was to get out of here in one piece. He cut a five-foot length of rope, and looped it about one hand. Replacing the two throwing stars in his vest pocket, Ki made for the door. He pressed his ear against it first, to listen for anyone immediately outside. He heard nothing. Then he turned the knob noiselessly and cracked the door. Again, nothing. Sticking his head out, he saw that he was in the clear.

To his right, Ki saw a stairway. There were other rooms on this floor, but the doors were all closed. Stepping quickly, lightly, on the balls of his feet, he went to the stairs. Taking a deep breath, he began to descend, step by step, bent low to see what was coming. About halfway down the stairs, he heard movement above him. He froze.

A door opened, then closed. It was down the hallway from the room where he had been kept. He was glad he had thought to close the door to that room—it might buy him a few precious seconds now. His breathing shallow, Ki retraced his steps, moving up the stairs. He heard the man move closer.

Unlooping the length of rope that he had taken with him, Ki took an end in each hand and held it taut, raised to chest level. The man moved across the landing, toward the room where Ki had been held. Without noticing the samurai at his back, the man went to the door. Just as his hand reached for the doorknob, Ki stepped up behind him and swung the rope around the man's neck and jerked it tight.

The man let out a strangled cry and his hands went to the rough rope that burned his neck. But Ki kept the rope at a killing tension, choking off air to the man's lungs. The man, a big, strapping fellow who smelled bad, went red in the face, his mouth hanging open gasping desperately for air. The samurai stabbed a knee into the man's back, causing him to quit struggling. The pain must have been excruciating, but Ki could not care about that. His own hands burned as he gripped the garotte, forcing the man down.

The man's knees buckled and he went to the floor with a loud thump. Ki kept the noose around his neck for another half minute, until he felt the man's whole body go limp. Then, quickly, he released the man, whose head hit the floor with another thump.

From below he heard someone call upstairs, "You all right, Carroll?"

When there was no response, the voice called again, "What's going on up there?"

Ki went to the stairway and, clinging to the wall, scurried down. He heard a shuffling of feet to his left, so he turned right, slipping around a corner into a darkened room. He had to fight to control his breathing, quietly gasping for air, as he heard somebody clatter up the stairs. He had only seconds to act. Where should he go? If he went outside, he was helpless—in the cold and in an unknown direction from Kansas City. If he stayed in the house, they would find him eventually and confine him even more securely than before. Still, he might be able to take out another man before they recaptured him—and that would be something.

From the second floor a man shouted, "Carroll is down! The Chinaman got him!"

Outside the house, near the back door, Jessie and Deighton heard the shout. She looked at him and, wordlessly, they agreed to go in. They went to the door and forced it open with a crash. They were in the pantry. It was dark and they fumbled their way into the kitchen. Empty. Throughout the rest of the house they heard the sound of men moving heavily from room to room.

"They've got Ki!" Jessie breathed. "He's here somewhere. We've got to find him—fast."

"We've also got to be careful we don't get killed," Deighton whispered hoarsely. "We still don't know how many men we're up against. Sounds like three or four moving around."

Then someone called, "Manley! The prisoner's gone! The room is empty!"

The reply was, "Find him, damn it!" Manley was still in the sitting room.

"They're all armed," Jessie reminded Deighton.

The big cattleman didn't need to be reminded; he kept his body between Jessie and the source of the commotion. "Stick close to me," he said. "Don't get separated."

With her big Winchester at the ready, she advanced, just a step behind Deighton. From the kitchen they went into a narrow, dark passage that turned sharply to the left, into a brightly lit opening—the dining room. But there was no one there.

Meanwhile, Ki was stuck where he was, with no chance to make a break for it. Not knowing that Jessie and Deighton were in the house, he was unable to devise any strategy to get to them. And he, too, was unaware of exactly how many men were left on guard, but he guessed that there were three, not counting the downed Carroll.

There was no time to make any plans. Ki heard someone approaching. The unseen man was moving slowly, coming down the stairs. Ki saw his opportunity. He waited for the man to reach the foot of the stairs. Then, suddenly, he stepped out and delivered a snapping blow with the edge of his hand to the base of the man's skull. The man's eyes rolled back in his head and he crumpled. He lay on the floor, an inert lump, as Ki raced toward the back of the house.

Jessie and Deighton advanced into the brightly illuminated dining room. They saw no one. Then, suddenly, a man appeared to their right. He carried a double-barreled scattergun. Jessie hit the floor and Deighton fell back around the corner as the man unleashed a lethal blast of buckshot. The explosion filled the room. Deighton swung back into range, his own rifle lifted to his shoulder, and squeezed off a shot at the man. The man ducked away and the bullet spanged into the wall instead.

Jessie levered a cartridge into the chamber and raised her rifle. She aimed low and got off a quick shot. The enemy's leg was in sight, and her shot shattered his kneecap. With a loud howl, the man went down, squeezing the second trigger of his double-barreled shotgun as he did. Another explosion ripped through the house. This time the shot sprayed into a window, blowing it apart.

As he writhed there in a pool of blood, screaming, both Jessie and Deighton, hugging their weapons tightly, stepped around the downed man. Coming around the corner, Jessie spotted the man called Manley, the phony conductor. Already he had his revolver out, leveled at her and Deighton, and he was about to trigger off a shot.

In a split second, though, Ki appeared behind the gunman. Jessie saw the scene unfold as if in a dream. First there was Manley's gun, trained at her gut. Deighton, behind her, grabbed her by the waist to throw her aside; his long-barreled Springfield was leveled on Manley. But Ki was too quick for them all. She saw him flick his wrist in a quick motion, almost a blur.

A whirring *shuriken* sped through the air—invisible to the naked eye, so fast did it move. Manley's eyes went wide and white as the blade bit into the right shoulder of his gun arm. His revolver discharged just as the sharp, star-shaped weapon sawed through muscle and tendon. His impaired aim was wide, the hot slug just missing Jessie's head as Deighton forced her to the floor.

Deighton held his fire as he saw Ki behind Manley. Then he saw Manley fall, his eyes wild in pain, his gun clattering to the floor.

Ki leaped forward, over the fallen man, to Jessie. He went to her and helped her up. She hugged him to her. "Is there anyone else in the house?" she asked.

"I think we got them all," Ki replied.

Then she got a good look at her samurai companion and saw the cuts and bruises on his face and arms. "My God, what happened to you?" she gasped.

Ki managed a crooked smile. "Ran into some trouble back in town. By the way, do you know where we are?"

Deighton explained the location of the house, and how far outside of Kansas City there were. "It's a half-hour ride back."

First, though, the trio attended to the men in the house. One was dead—the one Ki had garotted upstairs—and the others were hurt badly. Jessie stopped the bleeding of the man she had shot, applying a tourniquet above the knee. Ki tied up the man he had encountered at the end of the stairs, while Deighton kept Manley in his gunsight.

Ki then retrieved the *shuriken* blade from deep inside Manley's shoulder. The gunman winced in pain, and went pale. A splash of water from the kitchen revived him, and Jessie bandaged the wound.

She wanted to curse this man—or kill him—for the trouble he had caused, but first she must find out what she could from him.

Deighton took the words from her mouth. "All right, mister, who the hell are you, and why were you holding Ki? Who ordered you to do it?"

"I'm not telling you anything," he replied defiantly. His clean-shaven face looked suddenly haggard and drawn. He was frightened, and in great pain.

Ki wanted to feel sympathy for him, but could not. He himself had been in this position only hours ago—though it hadn't been any vicious act on his part that had put him there, only the priest's evil greed. Ki would tell Jessie what she wanted to know about this man, but he wanted to see if the man could be made to spill his guts first.

Jessie said, "Look, mister, you'll talk. It's only a matter of time. We want to know who hired you to kidnap Ki and hold him. And why were you on that train the other day, dressed as a conductor?" She stood above him menacingly, wanting to strangle the bastard with her bare hands for all the trouble he had caused her.

"My name is Norman Manley, but that's all I'm going to say. I don't owe you any explanation for anything I've done."

"Who are the other two, the ones who are still alive?"

"Blanchard and Egan," he said, shifting uncomfortably on the floor. "I said I don't owe you—"

"By God, man, you certainly do!" Deighton roared. "And you'll start talking now or feel sorry that you didn't." He walloped Manley across the face with a cruel fist, feeling the sodden impact of flesh on flesh.

The man groaned in pain and blood trickled from the corner of his mouth. Jessie restrained Deighton. Even she felt something for this man. She couldn't explain it; perhaps she had seen enough brutality for one day, looking at Ki's bruises.

★

Chapter 11

In the end—perhaps out of sheer exhaustion—Manley talked. He explained, and Ki confirmed, that the priest, Albino Patetta, wanted to use Ki to get to Jessie. Why, Manley did not know.

"What about the attack on the train?" Jessie wanted to know.

"That was the priest, too. I usually work for Jason Weatherby, but he introduced me to the priest several days ago—said I should do what the padre said. I don't think Weatherby knew about the train attack. The priest ordered it."

"So Patetta knew all along that we were coming," Jessie breathed, incredulous.

Ki said, "He represents the cartel, Jessie. It's no accident that he's here."

Jessie whirled to face Manley. "Did Patetta say anything to you about his business here in Kansas City?"

"No, he never told me anything about that."

"Did he send you out to cause the stampede at the railroad yards?"

"I just followed orders. Yes, he sent us."

Deighton spat. "You'd kill a woman because the priest ordered you to?"

"I get paid to do what I'm told, and I don't ask questions."

"You're dirt," Deighton said.

Jessie put her hand on his arm. "Don't let him get to you, Patrick. He's harmless now. It's Weatherby and Patetta who will have to pay."

"By God, they will," he agreed angrily.

Ki said, "We must act quickly, before they get wind of this."

"The prince," Jessie breathed. "What if Patetta talks to the prince and—"

"Prince Klaus wouldn't say anything," Deighton assured her. "I doubt that the priest will go near him, anyway."

"But Klaus knows—somehow he might give it away that we are onto Patetta, and then the priest will be able to warn Weartherby, to prepare for us. We better get moving."

"What do we do with these men?" Deighton asked.

"Leave them here—tied securely," suggested Jessie. "They've done enough damage for one day. I don't want them to do any more."

Deighton and Ki made sure that the injured gunmen were secured. They wrapped the dead man in a blanket and brought him outside in the cold air. He'd get a proper burial tomorrow, but for now there were other things to worry about.

Outside, in a barn near the house, they found a horse for Ki. He also borrowed Manley's coat, to keep warm on the cold ride. Then, retrieving Jessie's and Deighton's mounts, they rode back at a gallop to Kansas City to confront their enemies.

Jessie's mind was racing. She was not in the least surprised to learn that the priest was involved with the hated cartel, or that Weatherby had "loaned" the gunmen to Patetta. The whole thing had begun to stink days ago, from the trouble on the train to Weartherby's stalling of her loan request, to the stampede at the yards, and now to Ki's kidnapping. The only thing that surprised her was that the harassment was handled more sloppily than usual cartel standards. Perhaps that was because the priest was new at this sort of thing. Well, she promised herself, this would be the last time Patetta had a chance to cross her.

They rode against a cold wind in the darkly shrouded night. Deighton led the way, since he knew the road, with Jessie right behind, and Ki bringing up the rear on his gray mare.

It took about twenty minutes for them to reach town, riding up to the Hotel President, where Jessie and Ki dismounted. Deighton came down off his horse, too, and the three huddled there in the street.

"Patrick, you and I should see Weatherby right away. Ki, why don't you go in and clean yourself up, get some rest, then we'll come for you later," Jessie said.

"No," the samurai replied. "I'll go to the priest. Right now. He won't be expecting me, probably won't be prepared."

"I don't know . . ." she hesitated, worried that he wasn't in top condition after his ordeal.

Deighton said, "I know what Ki means. You can't stop him, Jessie."

She looked at her longtime friend, her eyes misting. Then she went to Ki and hugged him. Having come so close to losing him, Jessie didn't want anything else to happen to this man, who was like a brother to her.

"All right," she conceded. "But be *careful.*"

"Yes, I've learned my lesson about being careful," Ki said with a smile.

When Jessie and Deighton went away with the horses, Ki returned to his room, washed his face, and changed his clothes. Carefully he fastened a black cloth headband around his forehead, to keep the hair out of his eyes. Then he opened a long wooden case lined with purple silk, and from it removed the long, curved *katana* in its black lacquered sheath. The *katana* was traditionally the chief weapon of the samurai. Ki's, though he rarely used it, was sharpened to a keen edge, and shone brightly in the lamplight as he inspected it. Then he inserted the sheathed sword through his belt, so that it rode along his left leg. He was ready now to face the priest.

Using the same rear entrance to the royal party's hotel that he had used earlier in the day, Ki stole up the stairs undetected. He made his way surefooted to Father Patetta's room, where he rapped three times on the door. At first there was no answer. It was late, and the priest might indeed be sleeping. Ki heard the rustle of cloth and a low whisper.

Then the priest called out, "Who is it?"

"Manley," Ki replied, deepening his voice.

"One moment, Signor Manley," the priest said.

Ki waited. The door opened a crack. Patetta, expecting to see his hired gunman, was incautious. This gave Ki enough time to jam his foot in the door just as the priest attempted to slam it shut. Ki relished the look of horror and astonishment on Patetta's face. The priest pushed hard, trying to shut the door, but Ki pressed firmly, his foot planted immovably, preventing the door from closing.

The cleric's face was beet-red as he pushed with all his strength, but to no avail. Ki then brought his body against the door, shoving it open and sending the priest sprawling onto the carpet. Patetta's cassock was partly unbuttoned, his hair uncombed. And on the couch in the sitting room of his suite was a nude girl, clutching her dress to her bosom.

"You did not expect me, Father," the samurai said with a gallant bow.

"Son of the devil, how did you get here?" the priest gasped.

"Ask your men, Manley and Blanchard. They are responsible. They allowed me to come and speak to you. We have unfinished business between us."

"I—I don't know what you're talking about," Patetta bluffed. He was hoping that the presence of the girl would somehow control Ki.

But Ki, knowing this, said to the frightened girl, "You may put your clothes on and leave." He found a gold eagle in his pocket and flipped it to her. "Here is payment for your time and trouble," he said. "This gentleman won't have the chance to pay you."

"What do you think was going on here?" the priest huffed, as if it weren't obvious to any fool.

"You don't have to pretend with me, Padre. I am a man, too. I know what is in the hearts of men. She's a pretty girl; I don't blame you." He was anxious to get down to business, so he hurried the girl along.

When she was gone, he said to the priest: "What made you think you could get away with it, Patetta? Your friends in the cartel must have promised you a nice reward if you could put Miss Starbuck out of the way."

"What are you talking about?" Patetta said. He was still on the floor, propped up on his elbows. Ki advanced on him and he shrank back.

"Don't be coy with me. You told me all about your connection, don't you remember? I listened carefully and kept my mouth shut. But you have failed, and now you must pay the price."

Slowly the priest regained his feet. He fastened the open buttons on his robe and smoothed his hair—as if it would make a difference. He looked Ki up and down, his eyes locking on the long-bladed *katana*. "You are threatening me, heathen."

"Yes, you might say that. But just a few hours ago you were doing the threatening. How does it feel? I didn't like it, and I expect you don't, either."

"What do you want? I will pay you, if that is what you wish. Those men—they are worthless, they let you get away. That proves to me that you are worth much more than they. Tell me, what is your price? I can arrange to pay you—"

"You can't buy your way out of this."

"Then—what do you intend to do?" The priest's dark eyes were darting in every direction as he attempted to figure a way out. His lips quivered.

"I intend to bring you to justice. You arranged to kidnap me, you were involved in the destruction at the railroad yards, and you set Jessie and me up on the train before we even got to Kansas City."

An angry cloud passed over Patetta's face. "You should have been killed then. I paid good money to those men. They promised me they could accomplish the task, but they failed. They will burn in hell for that."

"I didn't please your superiors, is that what you mean?"

The priest was shivering with impotent rage. If he could have strangled Ki, he would have. As it was, he stood there glaring, his eyes coals of hate and anger. "Yes. My superiors in Europe will be mightily displeased. They are determined to eliminate your Miss Starbuck—and they will pay much money to do it. They will reward the man who can bring her down, as well as her yellow-skinned friend."

Ki said, "Come on. We'll talk to the prince. I must tell him that you're going to spend the night in a city jail."

The priest did what he was told, and together they went down the hall to see His Highness, Prince Klaus.

• • •

Meanwhile, Jessie and Deighton had been admitted to Weartherby's home by a sleepy butler. It was long past midnight, and the house was dark. The butler agreed to summon Mr. Weatherby, but warned that his master was sleeping and might not agree to see them.

"Oh, he will see us," Jessie said. "Tell him Miss Starbuck and Mr. Deighton are here."

Skeptically, the old man climbed the steps, shooting suspicious glances at the two visitors. In several minutes he returned with the message that Mr. Weatherby would meet them in the study.

Jessie and Deighton waited there for what seemed an eternity, as the big old clock on the elaborate mantelpiece ticked away. Finally, Weatherby appeared, his steely gray hair combed neatly and a fancy, ankle-length silk robe fastened around his trim waist. In all, he looked the picture of the prosperous man just awakened from a deep, untroubled sleep.

Feigning ignorance, he said, "Well, what brings you two out at this hour? Is something wrong?" But his voice held a slight tremor, as if he knew exactly why they were here. He even attempted a tepid smile. None of it worked, though, as he could see from their faces.

"My friend Ki is safe and sound, Mr. Weatherby. No thanks to you or that conniving priest," said Jessie. "And I know all about Father Patetta's ties with the European business cartel that killed my father. Patetta, in fact, tried to kill Ki and me before we even arrived in Kansas City."

Weatherby's mouth fell open. "I swear to you, I didn't know a thing!" His eyes were shining with fear. "Why are you telling me this? I never knew he tried anything like that. I only . . . did business with him. He is the prince's representative. We—"

"You talked nothing but business," Jessie went on. "Don't bother lying, Weatherby. Who was responsible for the stampede at the holding pens? Who was going to profit from

Ki's abduction? And, by the way, why did you stall me when I came to you with my intention to invest in the stockyards? You knew that was a good deal. But you dragged your feet. Was it to keep me in town so both you and the priest could get what you wanted from me?"

"No. That's crazy, Miss Starbuck. I told you—my people were studying your proposal. As a matter of fact"—he fluttered his hands—"I was going to call you in tomorrow to tell you that we have agreed to finance your proposed stockyard purchase."

"Without the board of directors' approval?" she taunted him.

"I—surely you understand, Miss Starbuck—"

"She understands perfectly, Weatherby," Deighton said. "Just like I do. Only it didn't take her as long as it took me to realize you're a lying son-of-a-bitch who won't hesitate to stoop to anything for the sake of a dollar."

"You malign me, sir," the banker protested righteously.

"You've been caught out this time," Deighton pressed. "We're going to notify the law about your activities, and this time you'll have nowhere to hide, nobody to pay off. Because this time we have others who can testify against you. The priest, for one, and your hired guns—Manley, Blanchard, Egan. They'll sing like birds and send you to prison for life. Your days of cheating and ruining lives are over, mister."

The banker turned to Jessie, his eyes wild. "You cannot believe this young man's rantings, Miss Starbuck. Your relationship with me would prove otherwise. And your father and I did business for years. You can see that he's unbalanced. I don't know what is the basis of these accusations, but I can disprove them—and I shall!"

"Save your breath, Mr. Weatherby," said Jessie. "What Patrick says is true. The men who were holding Ki aren't going anywhere right now. It seems they were holding him at your house—surely that is more than just a coincidence. Is it possible you didn't know your own house was being used to shelter these criminals?"

"Of course I didn't know!" Weatherby blustered. But his act was wearing thin.

"This isn't getting us anywhere," Jessie said. "Enough talk. Patrick, I think we should take Weatherby in to the city jail. The police will take good care of him."

"I agree," the young man said. "Come on, Weatherby. Why don't you get dressed and we'll escort you downtown. Wear something warm. It's cold in those little jail cells."

"No—you cannot—I won't allow you to do this to me. You're both insane. Nobody can put Jason Weatherby behind bars. I have done nothing wrong. I must speak with my attorney."

"We'll send him down to talk to you in the morning," suggested Jessie. "I'm certain he'll be just as happy to see you as you will be to see him."

"This is preposterous!" The banker looked from Deighton to Jessie and back again. Then he lowered his voice, speaking smoothly, confidently. "Listen," he said, "I know that you two young people are angry about all of this. But there is no harm done, really. Perhaps if I were to arrange a large payment—er, two large payments—to each of your personal bank accounts, we could forget the whole thing. My bank can handle the transaction tomorrow. What do you say?"

"Get dressed, Weatherby," Deighton gritted.

The banker looked like a cornered polecat. Jessie could almost see him arching his spine, the hair standing up at the back of his neck. He rose from his chair, his face gone pale, his eyes blank.

"Yes," he said in a strange, hollow voice.

The young man accompanied Weatherby to the foot of the stairs, where the banker waved him away. "I do not need you to help me dress myself!" he snapped. Then he made his way slowly up the stairs, followed by his white-haired manservant.

Jessie looked around at the elaborate furnishings in the study, remembering the glittering table that Weatherby had set the night he had entertained the royal couple. The man had accumulated much wealth, that was for sure, but look at him now—caught out as a cheat and a liar and a conspirator. The humiliation of it was worse for him than the actual guilt. How often in the past had he bought his way out of tough situations? She could only guess, but she had an idea that he had done it many times.

Deighton returned and stood by her side. "We've got him, Jessie," he said.

"Yes, but it doesn't feel good. He's a pathetic man, Patrick. Did you see the look in his eyes when he knew we weren't bluffing and that we couldn't be bribed? It was like a child who knows he is going to be punished for stealing a piece of candy."

"I can't feel sorry for him. Not after what he did to my father," Deighton said. "He's only paying for what he has done to many people—not just you or me or my dad."

"Well, he'll be brought to trial, and a judge and jury will decide what is to be done with him." That was her only consolation in this mess—to see that Weatherby was brought to justice.

"It won't be easy to convict him, even with all the evidence," warned Deighton. "He still carries a lot of weight in this town."

"But that won't help him, with all the evidence against him. The gunmen, the priest, and I don't know who else is involved. Any jackass can see what he's been up to."

"I hope you're right," said Patrick Deighton. "I'd hate to see him get off this time."

"He won't," Jessie vowed firmly. "Once he's in that courtroom—"

She was cut short by the sound of a muffled explosion—a gunshot. She looked at Deighton. His eyes were wide with alarm.

"Oh, no," he moaned, bursting from the room and up the stairs, with Jessie close behind him.

There, in his bedroom, they found Jason Weatherby with a gunshot wound—the bullet had entered the right temple and exited in a gory mess from the back of his head. His pistol was still clutched in his hand.

The prince, too, had been roused from the comfort of his bed. Now he confronted Ki and the disheveled priest. "What is the meaning of this, Father?" he asked Patetta. Having been informed by Jessie of her suspicions he had tried to see the priest earlier, without success. Now that Ki had brought him in, he had a chance to question him directly.

"I know nothing of what this man is accusing me of," the priest lied. Ki had to give him credit, though, he lied boldly and without reservation; he'd do anything to save his own hide. "Whom would you believe, Your Highness, this foreigner or myself?"

"You are a foreigner in my country, Father, do not forget," the prince reminded him. "And together we are all foreigners in America."

That rebuke hit the priest like a slap in the face. He stood directly in front of the prince, who was arrayed in a soft smoking jacket, his glorious whiskers brushed and perfumed. He stood erect and regal, and he would not countenance any disrespect or untruth from a commoner—priest or not.

"You would be nothing without me!" the priest hissed back.

"I would be a prince, a member of the royal house. I have loved and trusted you, Albino, but you have betrayed me."

"Never!" the priest defended.

"You have been conducting financial arrangements behind my back, dealing with this group of businessmen, representing their interests and your own—instead of mine. Do not expect to walk away from this without paying for it. You are subject not only to God's law, but to mine as well."

"Your Highness," Ki put in, "he must face justice in this country for his crimes here. If you were to take him back to Europe, it would be difficult to compel him to return for trial here."

"I understand, Mr. Ki," the prince stated, with an imperial wave of his hand. "My family and I will be embarking upon our Grand Tour very soon. We will be traveling for several months. In the meantime I will leave Father Patetta in your custody. Within a reasonable amount of time, he will be brought to trial in Kansas City, will he not?"

Ki smiled. "He will indeed. That is good of you, Your Highness."

"I admire the American system of justice," said Klaus. "'Judged by a jury of your peers,' they say—do they not?"

The priest listened to this good-natured badinage with growing concern. The prince, his longtime meal ticket, was going to leave him to the American dogs—where he would be certain to be convicted and jailed for years. He couldn't bear the thought. There had to be something he could do, someone he could turn to. Now that Weatherby had also been nailed by this Starbuck woman, there was no place he could go.

Ki watched him, reading his thoughts. The samurai knew that Patetta would be scheming to escape, somehow.

But even Ki did not suspect the priest's next move. Spying a jeweled ceremonial sword that the prince wore on special state occasions, the black-robed priest lunged for it. It lay on a table beneath a tall mirror. Before Ki could react, Patetta had the sword and scabbard in his hands. Then, with a flash of steel in the room's bright light, he unsheathed the weapon—three feet of shining tempered steel.

With a sinister grin, the priest said, "You shall never take me. I am a free man!"

Ki stepped between the prince and the mad priest, unsheathing his own *katana* blade, throwing the lacquered scabbard aside. He pushed the prince back, giving the priest a wide berth.

Father Patetta held the sword in his right hand and assumed a classic European fencing stance, with his left hand raised at his ear, his feet well apart. Ki had encountered this style of fighting before; but instead of matching the style, he took his own *kenjutsu* stance. He held his sword with both hands, his upper body squared with the lower half, feet apart parallel to his shoulders.

The prince stumbled away with a shout of alarm. Luckily for him, the suite of rooms was large enough—this front room itself quite big—to allow him to get far away from the combatants.

Ignoring the cry of his royal mentor, Patetta advanced on Ki, brandishing the sword menacingly, his upright body moving quickly. Ki saw the flash of steel and the swirl of the priest's black soutane and stood his ground. He was not impressed by the man's obvious fighting skill, though it was strange for a man of the cloth. Nor was he frightened in the least by this unexpected turn of events. If he had to fight the priest, he would as soon fight him with his *katana,* the sword of the nobility, as any other way.

The priest's mouth was twisted with determination as he took two long steps at Ki. He swung the sword powerfully from the right side, but Ki blocked it and there was a clang of steel on steel as the two blades met. Quickly, Patetta thrust inward, but Ki again parried the stroke, pushing the enemy's sword away and jumping back.

Then, as the priest circled him, awaiting a chance to strike, Ki raised his long sword directly in front of his face. With a quick twist of his wrists he brought it around clockwise, in a full circle, then reversed the movement. The blade cut through the air with a deadly whisper as Ki whipped it around again and again, taking small steps toward the priest as he did so.

The priest gritted his teeth and let Ki advance.

The samurai brought the *katana* around now in a wide-arcing slice, his arms extended. The priest jumped out of the way as the sword hacked through air where his shoulder had been. Sword raised, Patetta engaged Ki's blade with a ringing crash. Again their swords locked. This time the priest pushed Ki away and followed through with two hard thrusts. Ki swung his torso first right, then left to avoid the killing blade, and brought his own sword down, slashing Patetta's away.

Regaining his equilibrium, Ki wasted no time in coming back at the priest. His intent was not to kill but to disarm his enemy. He wanted Patetta alive to go to trial with Weatherby. But the priest had the killing madness in his eyes: Ki had seen it before in desperate men. The disgraced cleric was cornered, trapped by his own greed. Having gone this far, he was willing to kill so that he could escape and try to rebuild his corrupt empire. Ki watched his eyes and his midsection for a clue as to which way he was going to go.

Taking his sword in both hands, the priest made a sudden lunge directly at the samurai. Ki raised his *katana* quickly and met Patetta's sword with a horizontal block. He looked at the Roman's tense face through the lower corner of the crossed blades. He saw there a mask of hatred, the muscles and veins standing out from the skull. It struck him then that he might have to kill the priest after all—perhaps Patetta was truly mad.

Ki ducked and dropped his *katana* and scythed the blade at Patetta's legs. He missed flesh but sliced cleanly through the black cloth of the soutane. He then rolled to his left, under a table, as the priest's sword came down, splintering the wood of the table. Emerging from the other side, Ki unleashed a powerful overhead slice, bringing his sword down over the priest's, pinning it there on the surface of the table.

For a long moment the two men's eyes were locked as if in mortal combat—the ultimate confrontation between two proud, unforgiving warriors. But Ki had won this meeting. The priest finally knew that. Before releasing his sword, he allowed his lips to curl up in what might pass for a smile.

"It is yours, yellow man," Patetta snarled.

★

Chapter 12

Deighton finished telling his father the story of the night before last. The older man listened solemnly, his fingers interlocked. He was sitting before the blazing fire. Outside it had turned ugly—a hard rain and a bitter wind were beating at the windows.

Jessie said, "Ki took the priest to the city jail after Prince Klaus forced him to confess his involvement with the cartel. He spilled his guts."

Ki nodded in agreement. It had been unpleasant to see the look of anger and disappointment on the prince's face, to see the once-proud priest reduced to begging for indulgence, for his very life—which wasn't granted.

The three of them sat near the old man, sipping brandy. As the fire crackled, it sent a flickering light and welcome warmth over them. They had eaten an elaborate dinner of wild turkey and summer corn and platters of vegetables and fruits, served with a tasty wine the old man kept in his cellar. Filled with food and talk, they now sat together enjoying a respite from the trouble of days past.

Mr. Deighton had taken the news of Jason Weatherby's death without a glimmer of emotion. All he said was, "I'm not surprised, son. There must have been a lot more he wanted to cover up, for him to take his own life."

The young man now looked at Jessie, her hair as bright as the fire, her eyes glowing like green jewels. She had filled in gaps in his story, giving the old man all the information he craved. For he wanted to know exactly what had happened, how all the events had tied together, and how they had climaxed in the final confrontations of the night before last.

He broke the silence now, asking, "What happens to the prince and his family?"

"They're setting out tomorrow on their Grand Tour, Mr. Deighton. They'll be traveling by train for the first leg, out into western Kansas. Prince Klaus is determined to see some real live Indians, or 'savages,' as he calls them."

Mr. Deighton laughed. "These Europeans have no idea, really, what life is like out West. If he had come on this tour thirty years ago, he would have seen some things that would have curled his hair."

"Do you miss those days, Dad?" young Deighton asked.

The old man smiled, his blue eyes taking on light and life. His wrinkles seemed to fade as he spoke. "Those days were awfully rough, son. We never knew from day to day if we'd live or die—if we'd win our fortunes or lose everything we owned. But that was the challenge of it, the beauty of it. We were building something—a new way of life—with our own bare hands. We could see it growing in front of our eyes. This city—we couldn't even imagine what it would one day become! All we knew was that we were building it, that we were working to make your lives"—he gestured at his young guests—"richer than ours could ever be." He paused and brought the brandy glass to his lips. "Yes, I miss those days," he admitted. "I still miss your mother, God rest her soul. But I still have much to live for."

Deighton regarded his father with affection and respect. "You did a good job, Dad."

"Thanks, Patrick. It was all for you. I'm just sorry your mother didn't live to see you all grown up. She would have liked you, too, Jessie," he said, turning to his beautiful young guest. "You're a lot like her."

Jessie acknowledged the compliment, raising her glass and saying, "You're a gallant man, Mr. Deighton. I wish Ki and I could stay here for another week or two just to hear you go on like that." She smiled, her white teeth gleaming.

The old man chuckled. "If I were Patrick, I'd do everything in my power to keep you around."

Patrick turned several shades of red. "Dad, please," he said.

"We do have to conclude our deal," Jessie reminded him. "I didn't come all the way to Kansas City just to meet two handsome men."

"You've got my bid. Do you accept?" Deighton asked her.

"As a matter of fact, I do," she replied. "And I've arranged with Roger Penland at Guarantee Trust to accept your payment on my behalf and apply it toward the purchase of a stockyard operation next door to your meat-packing plant. It looks like we'll be doing business together for a long time to come."

"I like that idea," young Deighton said. This time it was his turn to raise his glass. "To the loveliest business partner I could ever imagine," he toasted.

"Wait till the men at the Circle Star hear about this," Ki

put in. "All their work is going to pay off. They'll like it."

"They ought to," Jessie said. "I'm getting an excellent price for the beef, and now we'll have the means to purchase or broker other herds as they come into Kansas City and through our yard."

"You know, Jessie," said Patrick Deighton, "you're going to have to hire a man to put in charge of your stockyard operation. You can't run it from Texas, by post or telegraph wire. Somebody'll have to be here full time."

"I know," she concurred. "I've already been asking around."

"So you'll have to stick around for a while to interview prospects," he added.

She nodded, and looked from Patrick to his father. "Did you two talk about this before we came over?" she asked.

"Dad did mention something about it," Deighton said with a sly smile.

"I'll admit I would like to keep you around as long as possible," said Mr. Deighton.

"That's what Weatherby tried," she said. "And it didn't work well for him."

"An old man like me doesn't get many chances to talk cattle with such a pretty young gal."

"You'd better stop flattering me—both of you," Jessie insisted. "I know what you're up to. But I must return to Texas as soon as this thing is settled."

Mr. Deighton looked into the roaring fire. It warmed him, but not as much as she did. "You'll always be welcome here in my house, Jessie," he said. "I do want to see you again."

"You will, Mr. Deighton," she said.

The old man regaled them for a while longer with tales of his youth, of the pioneering days in this Missouri River town that had been carved from the wilderness, that had played host to every known type of human being—from preacher to pirate, from cowboy to criminal—for the past forty years. It clearly brought back good memories, and the three younger people sat and listened with fascination.

Finally, though, Jessie rose. "We've got to be getting back to the hotel." She looked out the window. "Seems the rain has stopped."

Patrick Deighton rose reluctantly and said, "If you have to go..."

Ki grasped Mr. Deighton's hand firmly. "It was very good to make your acquaintance, sir."

"And you, Mr. Ki," the old man replied. "You are a remarkable man."

Ki bowed and exited. Jessie came to the elder Deighton and bent to kiss him on the forehead. "I'll see you again before I leave," she promised.

"You'd better," he croaked. "Or I'll send my son to find you and drag you out here by your hair, like the Indians do. You thought you saw the last of kidnapping when you found your Mr. Ki? Well, you haven't seen anything yet." His eyes were moist as he looked into hers. "Choose a good man to oversee your stockyard, young lady. Somebody you can trust."

"I will, Mr. Deighton. Goodbye." She released his hand and turned to Patrick. "Time to go."

The ride back to town in Deighton's buggy was a cold one, and the three bundled up tightly against the howling wind. Jessie rode between the two men. They did not say much to each other. There wasn't much to say. Jessie put her hand in Deighton's as he guided the horses with the other.

Upon arriving at the hotel, Ki jumped out and helped Jessie down into the slippery street, then saw her to the safety of the sidewalk. He went to Deighton and shook the young American's hand. "Thank you and your father for a very nice meal. And thank you for helping Jessie find me.

I will appreicate that always."

"It was my pleasure, Ki," said Deighton. "Take care of yourself."

"Jessie, I must take care of some business at the prince's suite, before he and his family embark upon their trip."

"I understand, Ki," she said, her eyes twinkling. She watched him go, turned to Deighton, and said, "Ki's a good man, Patrick—unlike any other. I love him like a dear brother."

"Let's go inside. You'll catch the grippe out here." He put his big arm around Jessie and escorted her inside and up to her room.

Slowly she began taking off her clothes. He watched her, the undeniable need burning within him. He went to her and kissed her, touching the burning skin that was exposed to his fingers. She was smooth and white and warm—and his.

"I'm going to start interviewing men tomorrow morning," she said as he kissed her long, curving neck.

"Not for this job," Deighton breathed.

"No," Jessie breathed. "Not for this job. You've proven yourself to me."

"You bet I have," he said, his arms enveloping her now.

"Just be quiet and make love to me." She led him over to her bed and together they lay there. Feeling his strong body next to her, Jessie put everything else out of her mind. She slipped her dress off and it fell to the floor.

"God, you're beautiful," he told her.

"I'm yours, Patrick, I'm yours." Jessie Starbuck molded her body to his and felt his arms around her and knew that she was safe and Ki was safe and this man loved her and that was all that really mattered.

Watch for

LONE STAR
AND THE RIVERBOAT GAMBLERS

twenty-seventh in the exciting LONE STAR
series from Jove

coming in November!